The Story of Re

A Tale of the American Frontier

Edward Sylvester Ellis

Alpha Editions

This edition published in 2024

ISBN : 9789362928115

Design and Setting By
Alpha Editions
www.alphaedis.com
Email - info@alphaedis.com

As per information held with us this book is in Public Domain.
This book is a reproduction of an important historical work. Alpha Editions uses the
best technology to reproduce historical work in the same manner it was first
published to preserve its original nature. Any marks or number seen are left
intentionally to preserve its true form.

Contents

CHAPTER ONE BROTHER AND
SISTER—THE SIGNAL...- 1 -

CHAPTER TWO AN IMPORTANT
LETTER—SHUT IN..- 8 -

CHAPTER THREE CAUGHT FAST—
A FRIEND IN NEED ....- 16 -

CHAPTER FOUR THE
CONSULTATION—ON THE ROOF ....- 24 -

CHAPTER FIVE A STRANGE VISIT—
OMINOUS SIGNS ....- 32 -

CHAPTER SIX THE MUDDY CREEK
BAND—THE TORCH..- 41 -

CHAPTER SEVEN "A LITTLE CHILD
SHALL LEAD THEM."—
SURROUNDED BY PERIL...- 49 -

CHAPTER EIGHT TALL BEAR AND
HIS WARRIORS—A SURPRISING
DISCOVERY...- 56 -

CHAPTER NINE NAT TRUMBULL
AND HIS MEN—OUT IN THE NIGHT ....- 64 -

CHAPTER TEN AN OLD FRIEND—
SEPARATED ....- 72 -

CHAPTER ELEVEN AT THE LOWER CROSSING—TALL BEAR'S LAST FAILURE..- 81 -

CHAPTER TWELVE CONCLUSION ....- 90 -

CHAPTER ONE

BROTHER AND SISTER—THE SIGNAL

IT is within my memory that Melville Clarendon, a lad of sixteen years, was riding through Southern Minnesota, in company with his sister Dorothy, a sweet little miss not quite half his own age.

They were mounted on Saladin, a high-spirited, fleet, and good-tempered pony of coal-black color. Melville, who claimed the steed as his own special property, had given him his Arabian name because he fancied there were many points of resemblance between him and the winged coursers of the East, made famous as long ago as the time of the Crusades.

The lad sat his horse like a skilled equestrian, and indeed it would be hard to find his superior in that respect throughout that broad stretch of sparsely settled country. Those who live on the American frontier are trained from their earliest youth in the management of quadrupeds, and often display a proficiency that cannot fail to excite admiration.

Melville's fine breech-loading rifle was slung over his shoulder, and held in place by a strap that passed in front. It could be quickly drawn from its position whenever needed. It was not of the repeating pattern, but the youth was so handy with the weapon that he could put the cartridges in place, aim, and fire not only with great accuracy, but with marked rapidity.

In addition, he carried a good revolver, though he did not expect to use either weapon on the short journey he was making. He followed, however, the law of the border, which teaches the pioneer never to venture beyond sight of his home unprepared for every emergency that is likely to arise.

It was quite early in the forenoon, Melville having made an early start from the border-town of Barwell, and he was well on his way to his home, which lay ten miles to the south. "Dot," as his little sister was called by her friends, had been on a week's visit to her uncle's at the settlement, the agreement all round being that she should stay there for a fortnight at least; but her parents and her big brother rebelled at the end of the week. They missed the prattle and sunshine which only Dot could bring into their home, and Melville's heart was delighted when his father told him to mount Saladin and bring her home.

And when, on the seventh day of her visit, Dot found her handsome brother had come after her, and was to take her home the following morning, she leaped into his arms with a cry of happiness; for though her relatives had never suspected it, she was dreadfully home-sick and anxious to get back to her own people.

In riding northward to the settlement, young Clarendon followed the regular trail, over which he had passed scores of times. Not far from the house he crossed a broad stream at a point where the current (except when there was rain) was less than two feet deep. Its shallowness led to its use by all the settlers within a large radius to the southward, so that the faintly marked trails converged at this point something like the spokes of a large wheel, and became one from that point northward to the settlement.

A mile to the east was another crossing which was formerly used. It was not only broader, but there were one or two deep holes into which a horse was likely to plunge unless much care was used. Several unpleasant accidents of this nature led to its practical abandonment.

The ten miles between the home of the Clarendons and the little town of Barwell consisted of prairie, stream, and woodland. A ride over the trail, therefore, during pleasant weather afforded a most pleasing variety of scenery, this being especially the case in spring and summer. The eastern trail was more marked in this respect and it did not unite with the other until within about two miles of the settlement. Southward from the point of union the divergence was such that parties separating were quickly lost to view of each other, remaining thus until the stream of which I have spoken was crossed. There the country became so open that on a clear day the vision covered all the space between.

I have been thus particular in explaining the "lay of the land," as it is called, because it is necessary in order to understand the incidents that follow.

Melville laughed at the prattle of Dot, who sat in front of him, one of his arms encircling her chubby form, while Saladin was allowed to walk and occasionally gallop, as the mood prompted him.

There was no end of her chatter; and he asked her questions about her week's experience at Uncle Jack's, and told her in turn how much he and her father and mother had missed her, and what jolly times they would have when she got back.

Melville hesitated for a minute on reaching the diverging point of the paths. He was anxious to get home; but his wish to give his loved sister all the enjoyment possible in the ride led him to take the abandoned trail, and it proved a most unfortunate thing that he did so.

Just here I must tell you that Melville and Dot Clarendon were dressed very much as boys and girls of their age are dressed to-day in the more settled parts of my native country. Remember that the incidents I have set out to tell you took place only a very few years ago.

Instead of the coon-skin cap, buckskin suit, leggings and moccasins, of the early frontier, Melville wore a straw hat, a thick flannel shirt, and, since the weather was quite warm, he was without coat or vest. His trousers, of the ordinary pattern, were clasped at the waist by his cartridge belt, and his shapely feet were encased in strong well-made shoes. His revolver was thrust in his hip-pocket, and the broad collar of his shirt was clasped at the neck by a twisted silk handkerchief.

As for Dot, her clustering curls rippled from under a jaunty straw hat, and fluttered about her pretty shoulders, while the rest of her visible attire consisted of a simple dress, shoes, and stockings. The extra clothing taken with her on her visit was tied in a neat small bundle, fastened to the saddle behind Melville. Should they encounter any sudden change in the weather, they were within easy reach, while the lad looked upon himself as strong enough to make useless any such care for him.

Once or twice Melville stopped Saladin and let Dot down to the ground, that she might gather some of the bright flowers growing by the wayside; and at a spring of bubbling icy-cold water both halted and quaffed their fill, after which Saladin was allowed to push his nose into the clear fluid and do the same.

Once more they mounted, and without any occurrence worth the telling, reached the bank of the stream at the Upper Crossing. He halted a minute or two to look around before entering the water, for, as you will bear in mind, he had now reached a spot which gave him a more extended view than any yet passed.

Their own home was in plain sight, and naturally the eyes of the brother and sister were first turned in that direction. It appeared just as they expected. Moderate in size, built of logs somewhat after the fashion on the frontier at an earlier date, with outbuildings and abundant signs of thrift, it was an excellent type of the home of the sturdy American settler of the present.

"Oh, Mel!" suddenly exclaimed Dot, calling her brother by the name she always used, "who is that on horseback?"

Dot pointed to a slight eminence between their house and the stream; and, shifting his glance, Melville saw an Indian horseman standing as motionless as if he and his animal were carved in stone. He seemed to have reined up on the crest of the elevation, and, coming to a halt, was doing the same as the brother and sister—surveying his surroundings.

- 3 -

His position was midway between Melville and his house, and his horse faced the brother and sister. The distance was too great to distinguish the features of the red man clearly, but the two believed he was looking at them.

Now, there was nothing to cause special alarm in this sight, for it was a common thing to meet Indians in that part of the country, where indeed many of them may be seen to-day; but the lad suddenly remembered that when looking in the direction of his home he had failed to see any signs of life, and he was at once filled with a misgiving which caused him to swallow a lump in his throat before answering the question—

"Who is it, Mel?"

"Some Indian; he is too far off for me to tell who he is, and likely enough we have never seen him before."

"What's he looking at us so sharply for?"

"I'm not sure that he is looking at us; his face seems to be turned this way, but he may have his eyes on something else."

"Watch him! See what he is doing!"

No need to tell the lad to watch, for his attention was fixed upon the warrior. Just as Dot spoke he made a signal which the intelligent youth could not comprehend. He flung one end of a blanket in the air slightly above and in front of him, and, holding the other part in his hand, waved it vigorously several times.

That it was intended for the eyes of the brother and sister seemed beyond all question; but, as I have said, they did not know what it meant, for it might have signified a number of things. It is a practice with many Indians to use such means as a taunt to their enemies, but they generally utter shouts and defiant cries, and nothing of the kind was now heard.

Besides this, it was not to be supposed that a Sioux warrior (that, no doubt, being the tribe of the red man before them) would indulge in any such action in the presence of a single white youth and small girl.

"I don't understand it," said Melville, "but I'll be as polite as he."

With which, he took off his hat and swung it above his head. Then, seeing that the Indian had ceased waving his blanket, he replaced his hat, still watching his movements.

"The distance was too great to distinguish the features of the red man."

The next moment the Sioux wheeled his horse, and heading westward, galloped off with such speed that he almost instantly vanished.

The Indian had been gone less than a minute when Melville spoke to Saladin, and he stepped into the water.

The instant his hoof rested on dry land the youth struck him into a swift canter, which was not checked until he arrived at the house. While yet some distance, the lad's fears were deepened by what he saw, or rather by what he failed to see. Not a horse or cow was in sight; only the ducks and chickens were there, the former waddling to the water.

When Archie Clarendon made his home on that spot, a few years before, one of the questions he had to meet was as to the best way of guarding against attacks from Indians, for there were plenty of them in that part of the country. There are very few red men who will not steal; and they are so fond of "firewater," or intoxicating drink, that they are likely to commit worse crimes.

The pioneer, therefore, built his house much stronger than he would have done had he waited several years before putting it up.

It was made of logs, strongly put together, and the windows were so narrow that no person, unless very slim, could push his way through them. Of course the door was heavy, and it could be fastened in its place so firmly that it would have resisted the assault of a strong body of men.

By this time Melville, who had galloped up to the front and brought his horse to a halt, was almost sure that something dreadful had happened, and he hesitated a moment before dismounting or lowering Dot to the ground. She began twisting about in his grasp, saying plaintively—

"Let me down, Mel; I want to see papa and mamma."

"I don't think they are there," he said, again swallowing a lump in his throat.

She turned her head around and looked wonderingly up in his face, not knowing what he meant. He could not explain, and he allowed her to drop lightly on her feet.

"Wait a minute," he called, "till I take a look inside."

In imagination he saw an awful sight. It was that of his beloved parents slain by the cruel red men—one of whom had waved his blanket tauntingly at him only a few minutes before.

He could not bear that Dot should look upon the scene that would haunt her, as it would haunt him, to her dying day. He meant to hold her back until he could take a look inside; but her nimble feet carried her ahead, and she was on the porch before he could check her.

Saladin was a horse that would stand without tying; and, paying no heed to him, the youth hurried after his sister, seizing her hand as it was raised to draw the string hanging outside the door.

"Dot," he said, "why do you not obey me? You must wait till I first go in."

It was not often her big brother spoke so sternly, and there came a tear into each of the bright eyes, as she stepped back and poutingly waited for him to do as he thought best.

Melville raised his hand to draw the latch, but his heart failed. Stepping to one side, he peered through the narrow window that helped to light up the lower floor.

The muslin curtain was partly drawn, but he was able to see most of the interior. Table, chairs, and furniture were all in place, but not a glimpse of a living person was visible.

"He peered through the narrow window."

The emotions of childhood are as changeable as the shadows of the flitting clouds.

Dot was pouting while Mel stood irresolute on the small porch, and was sure she would never, never speak to the mean fellow again; but the instant he peeped through the narrow window she forgot everything else, and darted forward to take her place at his side, and find out what it was that made him act so queerly.

Before she reached him she stopped short with the exclamation—

"Oh, Mel! here's a letter for you!"

CHAPTER TWO

AN IMPORTANT LETTER—SHUT IN

ASTONISHED by the cry, young Clarendon turned his head and looked at his sister, who landed at his side that moment like a fairy. She was holding a sheet of paper in her hand. It was folded in the form of an envelope, and pencilled on the outside in bold letters were the words—

"Melville   Clarendon.
"In haste; read instantly."

He took the letter from his sister and trembled, as if from a chill, as he hurriedly unfolded the paper and read—

"MY DEAR MEL,—Leave at once! The Sioux have taken the war-path, and a party of their worst warriors from the Muddy Creek country have started out on a raid. They are sure to come this way, and I suppose the house will be burned, and everything on which they can lay hands destroyed. They are under the lead of the desperate Red Feather, and will spare nothing. A friendly Sioux stopped this morning before daylight and warned me. I gathered the animals together, and your mother and I set out for Barwell in all haste, driving the beasts before us.

"I feel certain of either finding you and Dot at my brother's in the settlement or of meeting you on the way, for I suppose, of course, you will follow the regular trail; but, at the moment of starting, your mother suggests the possibility that you may take the upper route. To make sure, I write this letter. If the Indians reach the building before you, they will leave such traces of their presence that you will take the alarm. If you arrive first and see this note, re-mount Saladin, turn northward, and lose not a minute in galloping to the settlement. None of them can overtake you. Avoid the upper trail, where it is much easier for them to ambush you; keep as much on the open prairie as possible; see that your weapons are loaded; make Saladin do his best; and God be with you and Darling Dot.— Your Father."

"He hurriedly unfolded the paper and read."

The youth read this important message aloud to Dot, who stood at his side, looking wistfully up in his face. She was too young to comprehend fully its meaning, but she knew that her parents had left for the settlement, and that her father had ordered Melville to follow at once with her.

"The bad Indians are coming," he added, "and if we stay here they will shoot us. I don't think," he said, glancing around, "that they are anywhere near; but they are likely to come any minute, so we won't wait."

"Oh, Mel!" suddenly spoke up Dot, "you know I forgot to take Susie with me when I went away; can't I get her now?"

Susie was Dot's pet doll, and the fact that she left it behind when making her visit to Uncle Jack's had a great deal more to do with her homesickness than her friends suspected. The thought of leaving it behind again almost broke her heart.

"I am sure mother took it with her when she went off this morning," replied Melville, feeling a little uneasy over the request.

"I'll soon find out," said she, stepping hastily towards the door.

He could not refuse her wish, for he understood the depth of the affection she felt for the doll, whose dress was somewhat torn, and whose face was not always as clean as her own. Besides, it could take only a minute or two to get the plaything, if it had been left in the house. Although his situation prevented his seeing anything in the rear of the building, he was sure the dreaded Indians were not yet in sight, and he desired to make a hasty survey of the interior of the house himself.

How familiar everything looked! There were the chairs placed against the wall, and the deal table in the middle of the room. Melville noticed that the pictures which had hung so long on the walls had been taken away. They were portraits of the members of the family, and the mother looked upon them as too precious to be allowed to run any risk of loss. A few other valuables, including the old Bible, had been removed; but the parents were too wise to increase their own danger by loading themselves with goods, however much they regretted leaving them behind.

Although there was an old-fashioned fire-place, the Clarendons used a large stove standing near it. Curiosity led Melville to examine it, and he smiled to find it still warm. The ashes within, when stirred, showed some embers glowing beneath. There was something in the fact which made the youth feel as though the distance between him and his parents had become less than a short time before.

"Strange that I took the upper trail," he said to himself, resuming his standing position, "and thereby missed them. It's the first time I have been over that course for a long while, and it beats me that to-day when I shouldn't have done so I must do it; but fortunately no harm was done."

It struck him that Dot was taking an unusually long time in the search for her doll. Walking to the foot of the stairs, he called to her—

"It won't do to wait any longer, Dot; we must be off. If you can't find your doll, it's because mother took it with her."

"I've found it! I've found it!" she exclaimed, dancing with delight; "I had hid it in the bed, where mother didn't see it; bless your soul, Susie!"

And Melville laughed as he heard a number of vigorous smacks which told how much the child loved her pet.

"I suppose you are happy now," remarked Melville, taking her hand, while he held his gun in the other, as they walked towards the door.

"Indeed I am," she replied, with that emphatic shake of the head by which children of her years often give force to their words.

Melville placed his hand on the latch of the door, and, raising it, drew the structure inward. He had lowered his arm and once more taken the hand of his sister, and was in the act of stepping outside, when the sharp report of a rifle broke the stillness, and he felt the whiz of the bullet, which grazed his face and buried itself in the wall behind him.

The lad was quick-witted enough to know on the instant what it meant; and, leaping back, he hastily closed the door, drew in the latch-string, and, leaning his rifle against the side of the room, slipped the bar in place.

He had hardly done so when there was a shock, as if some heavy body were flung violently against it. Such was the fact, a Sioux warrior having turned himself sideways at the moment of leaping, so that his shoulder struck it with a force sufficient to carry a door off its hinges.

"What's the matter?" asked the frightened Dot; "why do you fasten the door, Mel?"

"The bad Indians have come; they are trying to get into the house so as to hurt us."

"And do they want Susie?" she asked Melville, hugging her doll very closely to her breast.

"Yes, but we won't let them have her. Keep away from the window!" he added, catching her arm, and drawing her back from the dangerous position into which her curiosity was leading her. "Sit down there," he said, pointing to one of the chairs which was beyond reach of any bullet that could be fired through a window; "don't stir unless I tell you to, or the bad Indians will take you and dolly, and you will never see father or mother or me again."

This was terrible enough to scare the little one into the most implicit obedience of her brother. She meekly took her seat, with Susie still clasped in her arms, willing to do anything to save the precious one from danger, and content to leave everything to her brother.

The youth had not time to explain matters more fully to his sister, nor would it have been wise to do so; she had been told enough already to distress and render her obedient to his wishes.

Following the startling shock against the door came a voice from the outside. The words were in broken English, and were uttered by the Sioux warrior that had made the vain effort to drive the structure inward.

"Open door—open door, brudder."

"I will not open the door," called back Melville.

"Open door—Injin won't hurt pale-face—come in—eat wid him."

"You cannot come in; we want no visitors. Go away, or I will shoot you!"

This was a brave threat, but it did not do all that the lad hoped. Whether the assailants knew how weak the force was within the house the youth could not say. He was not without belief that they might think there were several armed defenders who would make an attack or siege on the part of the Sioux too costly for them to continue it long.

The first purpose of Melville, therefore, was to learn how strong the force was that had made such a sudden attack. It was too perilous to attempt to look through one of the four narrow windows lighting the large room where he stood, and which covered the entire lower part of the building, and he decided, therefore, to got upstairs.

Before doing so, he made Dot repeat her promise to sit still where she was. She assured him that he need have no fear whatever, and he hurriedly made his way to the rooms above.

Advancing to one of the windows at the front, he peered out with the utmost caution.

The first Indian whom he saw was the very one he dreaded above all others. He recognized him at the first glance by the cluster of eagle-feathers stuck in his crown. There were stained of a crimson red, several of the longer ones drooping behind, so as to mingle with his coarse black hair which streamed over his shoulders.

This was Red Feather, one of the most desperate Sioux known in the history of the border. Years before he was a chief noted for his daring and detestation of the white men. As the country became partly settled he acquired most of the vices and few of the virtues of the white race. He was fond of "firewater," was an inveterate thief, sullen and revengeful, quarrelsome at all times; and, when under the influence of drink, was feared almost as much by his own people as by the whites.

Red Feather was mounted on a fine-looking horse, which there is little doubt had been stolen from some of the settlers in that part of the country. He had brought him to a stand about a hundred yards from the building, he and the animal facing the house.

As the Sioux chieftain held this position the lad was struck by his resemblance to the horseman whom he and Dot noticed at the time they halted on the other bank of the stream.

"Red Feather, one of the most desperate Sioux."

This discovery of young Clarendon suggested an explanation of the sight which so puzzled him and his sister. The chief had descried them at the same moment, if not before they saw him. Inasmuch as the occupants of the building were absent, he must have thought they had gone off together, and he could not have believed that, if such were the case, any members of the company would return—the boy, therefore, had ridden part way back to learn what was to be fate of the cabin and property left behind. Red Feather had waved his blanket as a taunt, and then rode off for his warriors, encamped near by, with the purpose of directing them in an attack on the house.

It was a most unfortunate oversight that Melville did not make a survey of the surrounding country before entering his own home, for had he done so, he would have learned of his peril; but you will remember that his first purpose was not to enter his house, and in truth it was Susie, the little doll, that brought all the trouble.

The dismay caused by his unexpected imprisonment was not without something in the nature of relief.

In the first place, a careful survey of his surroundings showed there were only six Sioux warriors in the attacking party. All were mounted, as a matter of course, fully armed, and eager to massacre the settler and his family. You will say these were enough to frighten any lad, however brave; but you must remember that Melville held a strong position in the house.

Such a fine horse as Saladin could not fail to catch the eye of the dusky scamps, and at the moment Red Feather fired his well-nigh fatal shot at the youth three warriors were putting forth their utmost efforts to capture the prize.

But the wise Saladin showed no liking for the red men, and would not permit any of them to lay hands on him. It was an easy matter to do this, for among them all there was not one that could approach him in fleetness. He suffered them to come quite near, and then, flinging up his head with a defiant neigh, sped beyond their reach like an arrow darting from the bow.

Melville's eyes kindled.

"I am proud of you, Saladin," he said, "and if I dared, I would give you a hurrah."

He watched the performance for several minutes, the rapid movement of the horses causing him to shift his position once or twice from one side of the house to the other. Finally, one of the Sioux saw how idle their pursuit was, and, angered at being baffled, deliberately raised his rifle and fired at Saladin.

"Saladin showed no liking for the red men."

Whether he hit the horse or not Melville could not say, though the animal showed no signs of being hurt: but the lad was so indignant that he levelled his own weapon, and, pointing the muzzle out of the narrow window, muttered—

"If you want to try that kind of business, I'm willing, and I think I can make a better shot than you did."

Before, however, he could be sure of his aim, he was startled by a cry from Dot—

"Come down here quick, Mel! A great big Indian is getting in the house by the window!"

CHAPTER THREE

CAUGHT FAST—A FRIEND IN NEED

MELVILLE Clarendon was so interested in the efforts of the three Sioux to capture his horse, that for a minute or two he forgot that Dot was below-stairs. Her cry, however, roused him to the situation and truth, and he flew down the steps.

In fact, the little girl had had a stirring time. While she was too young to realize the full danger of herself and brother, she knew there were bad Indians trying to get into the house, and the best thing for her to do was to obey every instruction Melville gave to her.

It will be recalled that Melville had a few words of conversation with one of the Sioux outside the door, who asked to be admitted. After the youth's refusal, there was silence for a minute or two, and, supposing the Indian was gone, the lad hurried to the upper story to gain a survey of his surroundings.

But the warrior had not left. After the departure of Melville he resumed his knocking on the door, but so gently that no one heard him except Dot. In her innocence she forgot the warnings given to her, and, sliding off her chair, stepped forward, and began shoving the end of the leathern string through, so that the Indian could raise the latch. She had tried to raise it herself, but the pressure from the outside was so strong that the friction prevented.

"Pull the string, and the door will open."

"There!" said the little girl; "all you've got to do is to pull the string, and the door will open."

When the Indian saw the head of the string groping its way through the little hole in the door like a tiny serpent, he grasped the end, and gave it such a smart jerk that the latch flew up.

But, fortunately, it was necessary to do more than draw the latch to open the door. The massive bar was in place, and the Sioux, most likely with a suspicion of the truth, made no effort to force the structure.

But while he was thus employed Red Feather had slipped from the back of his pony and approached the house. He took the side opposite to that from which Melville was looking forth, so that the youth did not notice his action. He saw the idleness of trying to make his way through the door, and formed another plan.

With little effort he raised the sash in the narrow window on the right. About half-way to the top was a wooden button to hold the lower sash in place when raised. The occupants of the house used no care in securing the windows, since, as I have explained, they were too narrow to allow any person, unless very thin of figure, to force his way through them.

Red Feather seemed to forget that he had tried to take the life of one of the white persons only a few minutes before; but, since no return shot had come from within the building, he must have concluded the defenders were panic-stricken, or else he showed a daring that amounted to recklessness;

for, after raising the sash, he pushed the curtain aside, and began carefully shoving his head through the opening.

Now, the house being of logs, it was necessary for the chieftain to force his shoulders a slight distance to allow his head fairly to enter the room. This required great care and labor, and more risk on the part of the Sioux than he suspected—since he should have known that it is easier to advance under such circumstances than to retreat, and, inasmuch as it was so hard to push on, it was likely to be still harder to retreat.

Dot Clarendon, like her brother, was so interested in another direction that she failed for the time to note that which was of far more importance.

But the feeling that she and her brother were in a situation of great danger became so strong that she felt there was only One who could save them, and, just as she had been taught from earliest infancy, she now asked that One to take care of them.

Sinking on her chubby knees, she folded her hands, shut her eyes and poured out the simple prayer of faith and love to Him whose ear is never closed to the appeal of the most helpless. Her eyes were still closed, and her lips moving, when the noise made by Red Feather in forcing himself through the narrow opening caused her to stop suddenly and look around.

The sight which met her gaze was enough to startle the bravest man. The head and shoulders of a hideous Sioux warrior were within six feet of where she was kneeling. The Indian was still struggling but he could get no farther, and, as it was, he was wedged very closely.

It must have caused strange feelings in the heart of the wicked savage when he observed the tiny figure kneeling on the floor, with clasped hands, closed eyes, upturned face, and murmuring lips. It is hard to think there could be any one untouched by the sight, though Red Feather gave no sign of such emotion at the time.

The face of the Sioux was not painted, though it is the fashion of his people to do so when upon the war-trail. It could not have looked more frightful had it been daubed with streaks and spots, and Dot was terrified. Springing to her feet, she recoiled with a gasp, and stared at the dreadful countenance.

Red Feather beckoned as best he could for the little one to come nigh him.

It was at this juncture that Dot uttered the cry which brought Melville in such haste from the room above. He rushed down, loaded gun in hand, and it is stating the matter mildly to say that he effected a change in the situation. Startled by the sound of the steps on the stairs, Red Feather glanced up and saw the lad, his face white with anger, and a very dangerous-looking rifle in his hand.

"I'll teach you manners!" called out Melville, halting on reaching the floor, and bringing his weapon to a level; "such a rogue as you ain't fit to live."

"Poured out the simple prayer of faith and love."

As you may suppose, Red Feather was satisfied that the best thing for him to do was to leave that place as quickly as he knew how. He began struggling fiercely to back out, and he must have been surprised when he found he was fast, and that the more he strove to free himself the more firmly he became wedged in.

Seeing his predicament, Melville advanced a couple of steps, holding his weapon so that its muzzle was within arm's length of the terrified visage of the chieftain.

"I've got you, Red Feather!" said the exultant youth; "and the best thing I can do is to shoot you."

"Oh, Mel!" called Dot, running towards her brother, "don't hurt him, for that would be wicked."

I must do Melville Clarendon the justice to state that he had no intention of shooting the Sioux chieftain who was caught fast in such a curious way. Such an act would have been cruel, though many persons would say it was right, because Red Feather was trying to slay both Melville and his little sister.

But the youth could not help enjoying the strange fix in which the Indian was caught, and he meant to make the best use of it. It is not often that an American Indian loses his wits when in danger, but Red Feather, for a few minutes, was under the control of a feeling such as a soldier shows when stricken by panic.

Had he kept cool, and carefully turned and twisted about as required, while slowly drawing backward, he could have released himself from the snare without trouble; but it was his frantic effort which defeated his own purpose, and forced him to stop, panting and despairing, with his head still within the room, and at the mercy of the youth, who seemed to lower his gun only at the earnest pleading of his little sister.

It was no more than natural that the Sioux should have felt certain that his head and shoulders were beginning to swell, and that, even if the lad spared him, he would never be able to get himself out of the scrape, unless the side of the house should be first taken down.

It was a time to sue for mercy, and the desperate, ugly-tempered Red Feather was prompt to do so. Ceasing his efforts, and turning his face, all aglow with cold perspiration, towards the boy, who had just lowered the muzzle of his gun, he tried to smile, though the expression of his countenance was anything but smiling, and said—

"Red Feather love white boy—love white girl!"

It is hard to restrain one's pity for another when in actual distress, and Melville's heart was touched the instant the words were uttered.

"Sit down in your chair," he said gently to Dot, "and don't disobey me again by leaving it until I tell you."

"But you won't hurt him, will you?" she pleaded, half obeying, and yet hesitating until she could receive his answer.

Not wishing Red Feather to know his decision, he stooped over and whispered in her ear—

"No, Dot, I will not hurt him; but don't say anything, for I don't want him to know it just yet."

It is more than likely that the distressed Sioux saw enough in the bright face to awaken hope, for he renewed his begging for mercy.

- 20 -

"Red Feather love white folks—he been bad Injin—he be good Injin now—'cause he love white folks."

"Red Feather," said he, lowering his voice so as not to reach the ears of the other Sioux, drawn to the spot by the strange occurrence; "you do not deserve mercy, for you came to kill me and all my folk. There! don't deny it, for you speak with a double tongue. But *she* has asked me to spare you, and perhaps I will. If I keep away all harm from you, what will you do for us?"

"Love white folks—Red Feather go away—won't hurt—bring game to his brother."

Having rested a few minutes, the Sioux began wriggling desperately again, hoping to free himself by sheer strength; but he could not budge his head and shoulders from their vice-like imprisonment, and something like despair must have settled over him when all doubt that he was swelling fast was removed.

It was at the same instant that two of the warriors on the outside, seeing the hapless position of their chief, seized his feet, and began tugging with all their power.

They quickly let go, however; for the impatient sachem delivered such a vigorous kick that both went over backward, with their feet pointed towards the clouds.

"Red Feather," said Melville, standing close enough to the hapless prisoner to touch him with his hand, "if I help you out of that place and do not hurt you, will you and your warriors go away?"

The Sioux nodded so vigorously that he struck his chin against the wood hard enough to cause him some pain.

"Me go away—all Sioux go away—neber come here 'gin—don't hurt nuffin—hurry way."

"And you will not come back to harm us?"

"Neber come back—stay way—love white folks."

"I don't believe you will ever love them, and I don't ask you to do so; but you know that my father and mother and I have always treated your people kindly, and they have no reason to hurt us."

"Dat so—dat so—Red Feather love fader, love moder, love son, love pappoose of white folks."

"You see how easy it would be for me to shoot you where you are now without any risk to myself, but I shall not hurt you. I will help to get your head and shoulders loose; but I am afraid that when you mount your horse again and ride out on the prairie you will forget all you promised me."

"Neber, neber, neber!" replied the chieftain, with all the energy at his command.

"Oh, Mel!" called Dot "don't hurt him."

"You will think that you know enough never to run your head into that window again, and you will want to set fire to the house and tomahawk us."

The Sioux looked as if he was deeply pained at this distrust of his honorable intentions, and he seemed at a loss to know what to say to restore himself to the good graces of his youthful master.

"You are sure you won't forget your promise, Red Feather?"

"Red Feather Sioux chief—he neber tell lie—he speak wid single tongue—he love white folks."

"I counted five warriors with you; are they all you have?"

"Dey all—hab no more."

Melville believed the Indian spoke the truth.

"Where are the rest?"

"Go down oder side Muddy Riber—won't come here."

Melville was inclined to credit this statement also. If Red Feather spoke the truth, the rest of his band, numbering fully a score, were twenty miles distant, and were not likely to appear in that part of the country. Such raids as that on which they were engaged must of necessity be pushed hard and fast. Even if the settlers do not instantly rally, the American cavalry are quite sure to follow them, and the Indians have no time to loiter. The rest of the band, if a score of miles away, were likely to have their hands full without riding thus far out of their course.

"Well," said Melville, after a moment's thought, as if still in doubt as to what he ought to do, "I shall not hurt you—more than that, I will help you to free yourself."

He leaned his gun against the table near him, and stepped forward and placed his hands on the head and shoulders of the suffering prisoner.

"Oogh!" grunted Red Feather; "grow bigger—swell up fast—bimeby Red Feather get so big, he die."

"I don't think it is as bad as *that*," remarked Melville, unable to repress a smile, "but it will take some work to get you loose."

CHAPTER FOUR

THE CONSULTATION—ON THE ROOF

MELVILLE now examined the fix of the chieftain more closely. His struggles had hurt the skin about his neck and shoulders, and there could be no doubt he was suffering considerably.

Clasping the dusky head with his hands, the youth turned it gently, so that it offered the least possible resistance. Then he asked him to move his shoulder slightly to the left, and, while Melville pushed carefully but strongly, told him to exert himself, not hastily but slowly, and with all the power at his command.

Resting a minute or two, the attempt was renewed and this time Red Feather succeeded in withdrawing for an inch or two, though the effort plainly caused him pain.

"That's right," added Melville, encouragingly; "we shall succeed—try it again."

There was a vigorous scraping, tugging, and pulling, and all at once the head and shoulders vanished through the window. Red Feather was released from the vice.

"There, I knew you would be all right!" called the lad through the opening. "Good-bye, Red Feather."

The chief must have been not only confused and bewildered, but chagrined by the exhibition made before the lad and his own warriors, who, had they possessed any sense of humor, would have laughed at the sorry plight of their leader.

Stepping back from the window, so as not to tempt any shot from the other Sioux, all of whom had gathered about the chief, Melville found himself in a dilemma.

"Shall I take Red Feather at his word?" he asked himself; "shall I open the door and walk out with Dot, mount Saladin and gallop off to Barwell, or—wait?"

There is little doubt, from what followed, that the former would have been the wiser course of the youth. Despite the treacherous character of the Sioux leader, he was so relieved by his release from what he felt at the time was a fatal snare, and by the kindness received from the boy, that his heart was stirred by something akin to gratitude, and he would have restrained his warriors from violence.

Had Melville been alone, he would not have hesitated; but he was irresolute on account of Dot. Looking down in her sweet trustful face, his heart misgave him; he felt that, so long as she was with him, he could assume no risks. He was comparatively safe for a time in the building, while there was no saying what would follow if he should place himself and Dot in the power of Indians that had set out to destroy and slay.

Besides, if Red Feather meant to keep his promise he could do so without involving the brother and sister in the least danger. He had only to ride off with his warriors, when Melville would walk forth, call Saladin to him, mount, and ride away.

"If he is honest," was his decision, "he will do that; I will wait until they are only a short distance off, and then will gallop to the settlement."

"Come," said he, taking the hand of Dot, "let's go upstairs."

"Why don't you stay down here, Mel?"

"Well, I am afraid to leave you alone because you are so apt to forget your promises to me; and since I want to go upstairs I must take you with me."

She made no objection, and holding Susie clasped by one arm, she placed the other hand in her brother's, and, side by side, the two walked up the steps to the larger room, occupied by their parents when at home.

"Now," said Melville, speaking with great seriousness, "you must do just as I tell you, Dot; for it you don't the bad Indians will surely hurt you, and you will never see Susie again."

She gave her pledge with such earnestness that he could depend upon her from that time forward.

"You must not go near the window unless I tell you to do so: the reason for that is that some of the Indians will see you, and they will fire their guns at you. If the bullet does not strike Dot and kill her, it will hit Susie, and that will be the last of *her*. The best thing you can do is to lie down on the bed and rest."

Dot obeyed cheerfully, reclining on the couch, with her round plump face against the pillow, where a few minutes later she sank into a sweet sleep. Poor child! little did she dream of what was yet to come.

- 25 -

She was safe so long as she remained thus, since, though a bullet fired through any one of the windows must cross the room, it would pass above the bed, missing her by several feet.

"The chief and his five followers had re-mounted their ponies."

Relieved of all present anxiety concerning her, Melville now gave his attention to Red Feather and his warriors. That which he saw was not calculated to add to his peace of mind.

The chief and his five followers had re-mounted their ponies, and ridden to a point some two hundred yards distant on the prairie, where they halted, as if for consultation.

"Just what I feared," said the youth, feeling it safe to stand before the upper window and watch every movement; "Red Feather has already begun to repent of his pledge to me, and his warriors are trying to persuade him to break his promise. I don't believe they will find it hard work to change his mind."

But whatever was said, it was plain that the Sioux were much in earnest. All were talking, and their arms swung about their heads, and they nodded with a vigor that left no doubt all were taking part in the dispute, and each one meant what he said.

"Where there is so much wrangling, it looks as if some were in favor of letting us alone," thought Melville, who added the next minute—"I don't know that that follows, for it may be they are quarrelling over the best plan of slaying us, with no thought on the part of any one that they are bound in honor to spare us."

By-and-by the ponies, which kept moving uneasily about, took position so that the heads of all were turned fully or partly towards the building, from which the lad was attentively watching their movements.

During these exciting moments Melville did not forget Saladin. The sagacious animal, being no longer troubled by those that were so anxious to steal him, had halted at a distance of an eighth of a mile, where he was eating the grass as though there was nothing unusual in his surroundings.

"I hope you will be wise enough, old fellow," muttered his young master, "to keep them at a distance; that shot couldn't have hit you, or, if it did, it caused nothing more than a scratch."

The horse's wisdom was tested the next minute. One of the warriors withdrew from the group, and began riding at a gallop towards Saladin. As he drew near he brought his pony down to a walk, and evidently hoped to calm the other's fears sufficiently to permit a still closer approach.

Melville's heart throbbed painfully as the distance lessened, and he began to believe he was to lose his priceless animal after all.

"Why didn't I think of it?" he asked himself, placing his finger in his mouth, and emitting a shrill whistle that could have been heard a mile distant.

It was a signal with which Saladin was familiar. He instantly raised his head and looked towards the house. As he did so he saw one of his mounted enemies slowly approaching, and within a dozen rods. It was enough, and breaking into a gallop, he quickly ended all hope of his capture by *that* Sioux brave.

That signal of Melville Clarendon had also been heard by all the Sioux, who must have thought it was due to that alone that the warrior failed to secure the valuable animal. The youth saw the group looking inquiringly at the house, as if to learn from what point the sound came, and the expression on the dark faces was anything but pleasing to him.

He wished to give Red Feather credit for the delay on the part of the Sioux. Their actions showed they were hotly disputing over something, and what more likely than that it was the question of assailing the house and outbuildings?

But there were several facts against this theory. Red Feather held such despotic sway over his followers that it was hard to understand what cause could arise for any dispute with them about the disposal to be made of the brother and sister. If he desired to leave them alone, what was to prevent him riding off and obliging every one of his warriors to go with him?

This was the question which Melville continually asked himself, and which he could not answer as he wished, being unable to drive away the belief that the chief was acting a double part.

The Sioux had reached some decision; for, on the return of the one who failed to secure Saladin, they ceased disputing, and rode towards the window from which Melville was watching them.

Their ponies were on a slow walk, and the expression on their forbidding faces was plainly seen as their eyes ranged over the front of the building. The youth had withdrawn, so as to stand out of range; but, to end the doubt in his mind, he now stepped out in full view of every one of the warriors.

"Melville had warning enough to leap back."

The doubt was removed at once. Previous to this the lad had raised the lower sash, so as to give him the chance to fire, and as he stood, his waist and shoulders were in front of the upper part of the glass. It so happened that Red Feather and one of his warriors were looking at the very window at which he appeared. Like a flash both guns went to their shoulders and were discharged.

"He pointed his own weapon outward, and fired."

But Melville had enough warning to leap back, as the jingle and crash of glass showed how well the miscreants had aimed. Stirred to the deepest anger, he pointed his own weapon outward and fired into the party, doing so with such haste that he really took no aim at all.

It is not likely that his bullet had gone anywhere near the Sioux, but it had served the purpose of warning them that he was as much in earnest as themselves.

Melville placed a cartridge in the breech of his rifle with as much coolness as a veteran, and prepared himself for what he believed was to be a desperate defence of himself and sister.

It must not be thought that he was in despair; for, when he came to look over the situation, he found much to encourage him. In the first place, although besieged by a half-dozen fierce Sioux, he was sure the siege could not last long. Whatever they did must be done within a few hours.

While it was impossible to tell the hour when his parents started from Barwell, it must have been quite early in the morning, and there was every reason to hope they would reach the settlement by noon at the latest. The moment they did so they would learn that Melville had left long before for home, and therefore had taken the upper trail, since, had he not done so, the parties would have met on the road.

True, Mr. Clarendon would feel strong hope that his son, being so well mounted, would wheel about and follow without delay the counsel in the letter; but he was too shrewd to rely fully on such hope. What could be more certain than that he would instantly gather a party of friends and set out to their relief?

The great dread of the youth was that the Sioux would set fire to the buildings, and he wondered many times that this was not done at the time Red Feather learned of the flight of the family.

Melville glanced at Dot, and, seeing she was asleep, he decided to go downstairs and make a fuller examination of the means of defence.

"Everything seems to be as secure as it can be," he said, standing in the middle of the room and looking around; "that door has already been tried, and found not wanting. The only other means of entrance is through the windows, and after Red Feather's experience I am sure neither he nor any of his warriors will try *that*."

There were four windows—two at the front and two at the rear—all of the same shape and size. There was but the single door, of which so much has already been said, and therefore the lower portion of the building could not be made safer.

The stone chimney, so broad at the base that it was more than half as wide as the side of the outside wall, was built of stone, and rose a half-dozen feet above the roof. It was almost entirely out of doors, but was solid and strong.

"If the Indians were not such lazy people," said Melville—looking earnestly at the broad fire-place, in front of which stood the new-fashioned stove—"they might set to work and take down the chimney, but I don't think there is much danger of *that*."

He had hardly given expression to the thought when he fancied he heard a slight noise on the outside, and close to the chimney itself. He stepped forward, and held his ear to the stones composing the walls of the fire-place.

Still the sounds were faint, and he then touched his ear against them, knowing that solid substances are much better conductors of sound than air. He now detected the noise more plainly, but it was still so faint that he could not identify it.

He was still striving hard to do so when, to his amazement, Dot called him from above-stairs—

"Where are you, Mel? Is that you that I can hear crawling about over the roof?"

CHAPTER FIVE

A STRANGE VISIT—OMINOUS SIGNS

MELVILLE Clarendon went up the short stairs three steps at a time, startled as much by the call of his sister as by anything that had taken place since the siege of the cabin began.

As he entered the room he saw Dot sitting up in bed, and staring wonderingly at the shivered window-glass, particles of which lay all around.

"Oh, Mel!" said she, "papa will scold you for doing that; how came you to do it?"

"It was the bad Indians who fired through the window at me, and I fired at them: you were sleeping so soundly that you only half awoke; but you must keep still a few minutes longer."

"I thought that was you on the roof," she added, in a lower voice.

That there was someone overhead was certain. The rasping sound of a person moving carefully along the peak of the roof was audible. The lad understood the meaning of that which puzzled him when on the lower floor: one of the warriors was carefully climbing the chimney—a task not difficult, because of its rough uneven formation.

The significance of such a strange act remained to be seen. It appeared unlikely that any of the Sioux were daring enough to attempt a descent of the chimney; but that such was really his purpose became clear within the following minute.

The Indian, after making his way a short distance along the peak, returned to the chimney, where, from the noises which reached the listening ones, it was manifest that he was actually making his way down the flue, broad enough to admit the passage of a larger body than himself.

"I won't be caught foul *this* time," said Melville, turning to descend the stairs again; "Dot, stay right where you are on the bed till I come back or call to you."

She promised to obey, and there could be no doubt that she would do so.

"They must think I'm stupid," muttered the youth, taking his position in the middle of the room, with his rifle cocked and ready for instant use; "but they will find out the idiot is some one else."

He had not long to wait when in the large open space at the back of the stove appeared a pair of moccasins groping vaguely about for support. The pipe from the stove, instead of passing directly up the chimney, entered it by means of an elbow. Had it been otherwise, the daring warrior would have found himself in a bad fix on arriving at the bottom.

It would have been idle for the young man standing on the watch to fire at the feet or legs, and he waited an instant, when the Indian dropped lightly on his feet, and, without the least hesitation, stepped forward in the apartment and confronted Melville.

The latter was dumbfounded, for the first glance at his face showed that he was the chieftain Red Feather, the Indian whom of all others he least expected to see.

The act of the savage was without any possible explanation to the astonished youth, who, recoiling a step, stared at him, and uttered the single exclamation—

"Red Feather!"

"Howly do, broder?" was the salutation of the Sioux, whose dusky face showed just the faintest smile.

Red Feather's descent of the chimney had not been without some disagreeable features. His blanket and garments, never very tidy, were covered with soot, enough of which had got on his face to suggest that he had adopted the usual means of his people to show they were on the war-path.

"A pair of moccasins groping vaguely about for support."

His knife and tomahawk were thrust in his girdle at his waist, and throughout this laborious task he had held his rifle fast, so that he was fully armed.

"Howly do?" he repeated, extending his hand, which Melville was too prudent to accept.

"No," he replied, compressing his lips, and keeping his finger on the trigger of his gun, "Red Feather speaks with a double tongue; he is not our friend."

"Red Feather been bad Injin—want white folks' scalp—don't want 'em now—little pappoose pray to Great Spirit—*dat* make Red Feather feel bad—he hab pappoose—he lub Injin pappoose—lub white pappoose—much lub white pappoose."

This remark shed light upon the singular incident. To Melville it was a mystery beyond understanding that any person could look upon the sweet innocent face of Dot without loving her. Knowing how vile an Indian Red Feather had been, it was yet a question with the youth whether he could find it in his heart to wish ill to his wee bit of a sister.

Was it unreasonable, therefore, to believe that this savage warrior had been touched by the sight of the little one on her knees, with her hands clasped in prayer, and by her eagerness to keep away all harm from him?

This theory helped to explain what took place after the release of Red Feather from his odd imprisonment. The five warriors whom he had brought with him upon his raid must have combated his proposal to leave the children unharmed. In the face of his savage overbearing disposition they had fought his wish to keep the pledge to them, while he as firmly insisted upon its fulfilment.

But if such were the fact, how could his descent of the chimney be explained?

Melville did not try to explain it, for he had no time just then to speculate upon it; the explanation would come shortly.

The youth, however, was too wise to act upon that which he hoped was the truth. He had retreated nearly to the other side of the room, where he maintained the same defiant attitude as at first.

Red Feather read the distrust in his face and manner. With a deliberation that was not lacking in dignity, he walked slowly to the corner of the apartment, Melville closely following him with his eye, and leaned his gun against the logs. Then he drew his knife and tomahawk from his girdle, and threw them on the floor beside the more valuable weapon. That done, he moved back to the fire-place, folded his arms, and, fixing his black eyes on the countenance of the lad, repeated—"Red Feather friend of white folk."

"I believe you," responded Melville, carefully letting down the hammer of his rifle and resting the stock on the floor; "now I am glad to shake hands with you."

A broader smile than before lit up the dusky face as the chief warmly pressed the hand of the youth, who felt just a little trepidation when their palms met.

"Where pappoose?" asked Red Feather, looking suggestively at the steps leading to the upper story.

"Dot!" called Melville, "come down here; someone wants to see you."

The patter of feet was heard, and the next instant the little one came tripping downstairs, with her doll clasped by one arm to her breast.

"Red Feather is a good Indian now, and he wants to shake hands with you."

With a faint blush and a sweet smile Dot ran across the floor and held out her tiny hand. The chieftain stooped, and not only took the palm of the little girl, but placed each of his own under her shoulders and lifted her from the floor. Straightening up, he touched his dusky lips to those of the innocent one, murmuring, with a depth of emotion which cannot be described—

"Red Feather lub white pappoose—she make him good Injin—he be her friend always."

The chieftain touched his lips but once to those of the little one, who showed no hesitation in accepting the salute. Pure, innocent, and good herself, she had not yet learned how evil the human heart may become.

Not only did she receive the salute willingly, but threw her free arm around the neck of the Indian and gave him a kiss.

"Red Feather, what made you come down the chimney?" questioned Melville when the Indian had released his sister.

"Can't come oder way," was the instant response.

"True; but why do you want to enter this house?"

"Be friend of white folk—come tell 'em."

"I am sure of that; but what can you do for us?"

Red Feather gave no direct answer to this question, but walked upstairs. As he did so he left every one of his weapons on the lower floor, and by a glance cast over his shoulder expressed the wish that the brother and sister should follow him. They did so, Dot tripping ahead, while Melville retained his weapons.

Reaching the upper floor, the Sioux walked directly to the window through which the shots had come that shattered the two panes of glass.

There was a curious smile on his swarthy face as he pointed at the pane on the left, and said—

"Red Feather fire *dat!*"

The explanation of his remark was that had Melville kept his place in front of the window at the moment the rifles were discharged, only one of the bullets would have hit him, and that would have been the one which Red Feather did not fire.

"'She make him good Injin—he be her friend always.'"

The shot which he sent into the apartment, and which filled the youth with so much indignation, had been fired for the purpose of making the other warriors believe the chieftain was as bitter an enemy of the brother and sister as he was of all white people.

Having convinced his followers on this point, he made his position still stronger with them by declaring his purpose of descending the chimney, and having it out with them, or rather with the lad, within the building.

Red Feather peered out of the window, taking care that none of his warriors saw him, though they must have felt a strong curiosity to learn the result of his strange effort to overcome the little garrison. Melville supposed that he had arranged to communicate with them by signal, for the result of the attempt must be settled quickly.

The youth took the liberty of peeping forth from the other window on the same side of the house.

Only two of the Sioux were in their field of vision, and their actions did not show that they felt much concern for their chief. They were mounted on their horses, and riding at a walk towards the elevations from which Red Feather had waved his blanket to the brother and sister when on the other side of the stream.

Melville's first thought was that they had decided to leave the place, but that hope was quickly dispelled by the action of the warriors. At the highest point of the hill they checked their ponies, and sat for a minute gazing fixedly to the northward in the direction of the settlement.

"They are looking for our friends," thought the youth, "but I am afraid they will not be in sight for a good while to come."

At this juncture one of the warriors deliberately rose to a standing position on the back of his pony, and turned his gaze to the westward.

"Now they are looking for *their* friends," was the correct conclusion of Melville, "and I am afraid they see them; yes, there is no doubt of it."

The warrior, in assuming his delicate position, passed his rifle to his companion, whose horse was beside him. Then, with his two hands free, he drew his blanket from around his shoulders and began waving it, as Red Feather had done earlier in the day.

Melville glanced across at Red Feather, who was attentively watching the performance. He saw the countenance grow more forbidding, while a scowl settled on his brow.

It was easy to translate all this. The Sioux had caught sight of some of their friends, and signalled them. This would not have been done had there not been some person or persons to observe it.

The party which the chieftain had described as being in the Muddy Creek country must have changed their course and hastened to join Red Feather and the smaller party. If such were the fact, they would arrive on the spot within a brief space of time.

The interesting question arose whether, in the event of such arrival, and the attack that was sure to follow, Red Feather would come out as open defender of the children against his own people. Had there been only the five original warriors, he might have played a part something akin to neutrality, on the ground that his descent of the chimney had turned out ill for him, and, being caught at disadvantage he was held idle under the threat of instant death. Still further, it might have been his province to assume the character of hostage, and thus to defeat the overthrow of the couple by the Sioux.

But the arrival of the larger party would change everything. Among the Muddy Creek band were several who disliked Red Feather intensely enough to be glad of a chance to help his discomfiture.

He had agreed that, in the event of his surprising the lad who was making such a brave defence, he would immediately appear at the front window and announce it, after which he would unbar the door and admit the warriors to the "last scene of all."

"'Let the Sioux send more of his warriors down the chimney!'"

Several minutes had now passed, and no such announcement was made. The other three Sioux were lingering near the building, awaiting the signal which came not.

While the two were engaged on the crest of the hill the others suddenly came round in front of the house. They were on foot, and looked inquiringly at the windows, as if at a loss to understand the cause of the silence. Red Feather instantly drew back, and said in a low voice to Melville—

"Speak to Injin—dem tink Red Feather lose scalp."

Grasping the situation, the youth showed himself at the window, where the Sioux were sure to see him, and uttered a tantalizing shout.

"Let the Sioux send more of their warriors down the chimney!" he called out; "the white youth is waiting for them, that he may take their scalps."

This was followed by another shout, as the lad withdrew beyond reach of a rifle-ball, that left no doubt of its meaning on the minds of the astounded warriors.

CHAPTER SIX

THE MUDDY CREEK BAND—THE TORCH

IT was easy for any spectator to interpret the actions and signals of the Sioux warrior who was standing erect on his pony and waving his blanket at some party invisible to the others.

After a minute or two he rested, with the blanket trailing beside him, while he still held his erect position, and continued gazing earnestly over the prairie. This showed that he was waiting for an answer to his signal. Either there was none, or that which was given was not satisfactory, for up went the blanket once more, and he swung it more vigorously than before, stopping and gazing away again.

This time the reply was what was desired, for the warrior dropped as suddenly astride of his horse as though his feet had been knocked from under him, and, wheeling about, he and his companion galloped down the hill to where the others were viewing the cabin.

The taunting words which Melville had called through the front window must have convinced the Sioux that the pitcher had gone once too often to the fountain. Red Feather had escaped by a wonderful piece of good fortune when wedged in the window, and had been encouraged to another attempt, which ended in his ruin.

"Red Feather," said Melville, stepping close to the chieftain, who was still peering through one of the windows, "the other Sioux will soon be here."

"Dat so—dat so," replied the Indian, looking around at him and nodding his head several times.

"What will they do?"

"Standing erect and waving his blanket."

Instead of replying to this question the chief seemed to be plunged in thought. He gazed fixedly in the face of the youth, as if uncertain what he ought to answer, and then he walked to the head of the stairs.

"Wait here—don't come."

And, without anything more, he went down the steps slowly, and without the slightest noise. Melville listened, but could hear nothing of his footfalls, though certain that he was moving across the floor.

"I don't like this," muttered the lad, compressing his lips and shaking his head; "it makes me uneasy."

He was now in the lower story, where he left his rifle, knife, and tomahawk. He was therefore more fully armed than the youth, and, if he chose to play the traitor, there was nothing to prevent it.

It seemed to Melville that the coming of the larger party was likely to change whatever plans Red Feather might have formed for befriending him and his sister. What more probable than that he had decided to return to his first love?

But speculation could go on this way for ever, and without reaching any result.

"I'll do as I have done all along," he muttered; "I'll trust in Heaven and do the best I can. I'm sure of one thing," he added; "whatever comes, Red

Feather won't hurt Dot: he has spared me on her account: and if he turns against me now, he will do what he can to save her. Therefore I'll make use of the little one."

Dot had held her peace through these trying moments, but he now called her to him and explained what he wished her to do. It was that she should place herself at the head of the stairs and watch Red Feather. In case he started to open the door, or to come up the stairs, she was to tell him. Dot was beginning to understand more clearly than before the situation in which she was placed. The belief that she could be of some use to her brother made her more anxious than ever to do her part. She walked to the head of the stairs and sat down where she could see what went on below.

Returning to his place at the window, Melville found enough to interest him without thinking of Red Feather.

"The whole party broke out in a series of yells."

The band from the Muddy Creek country had just arrived, and as nearly as he could judge, there were fully a score—all wild, ugly-looking fellows, eager for mischief. They had just galloped up the hill, where they gathered round the man that had first signalled them, he having ridden forward to meet them. They talked for several minutes, evidently to learn what had taken place in and around the Clarendon cabin.

This was soon made clear to them, and then the whole party broke into a series of yells enough to startle the bravest man. At the same time they began riding rapidly back and forth, swinging their rifles over their heads, swaying their bodies first on one side and then on another, and apparently growing more excited every minute.

At first they described short circles on the prairie, and then suddenly extended them so as to pass entirely around the house.

The Sioux, as they came in sight in front of the cabin, were in such a fire range that the youth felt sure he could bring down a warrior at every shot. He was tempted to do so, but restrained himself.

He reflected that, though several shots had been fired, no one, so far as he knew, had been hurt on either side. He had brought his own rifle to his shoulder more than once, and but a feather's weight more pressure on the trigger would have discharged it, but he was glad he had not done so.

"I shall not shoot any one," he said, determinedly, "until I see it must be done for the sake of Dot or myself. I wonder what Red Feather is at?"

Dot was still sitting at the head of the stairs, dividing her attention between Susie her doll and the chieftain. Stepping softly toward her, Melville asked—

"What is he doing, Dot?"

"Nothing."

"Where is he standing?"

"Beside the front window, looking out just like you did a minute ago."

This was reassuring information, and helped to drive away the fear that had troubled the youth ever since the Sioux passed below stairs.

"Mel," called his sister the next minute, "I'm awful hungry; ain't it past dinner-time?"

"I'm afraid there is nothing to eat in the house."

"I'm awful thirsty, too."

"I feel a little that way myself, but I don't believe there is anything to eat or drink. You know, father and mother didn't expect us to stay here, or they would have left something for us."

"Can't I go downstairs and look?"

"Yes, if you will keep away from the windows, and tell Red Feather what you are doing."

"Hasn't he got eyes that he can see for himself?" asked the little one as she hurried down the steps.

The chief looked around when he heard the dainty steps, wondering what errand brought her downstairs.

"Red Feather," said the young lady, "I'm hungry; ain't you?"

"No—me no hungry," he answered, his dark face lighting up with pleasure at sight of the picture of innocence.

"Then you must have eaten an awful big breakfast this morning," remarked Dot, walking straight to the cupboard in the farther corner of the room, into which Melville had glanced when he first entered the house; "I know where mother keeps her jam and nice things."

That she knew where the delicacies were stored Dot proved the next minute, when, to her delight, she found everything that heart, or rather appetite, could wish.

There were a jar of currant jam, a pan of cool milk, on which a thick crust of yellow cream had formed, three-fourths of a loaf of bread, and an abundance of butter. Good Mrs. Clarendon left them behind because she had an abundance without them. Little did she dream of the good service they were destined to do.

Dot uttered such a cry of delight that the chief walked toward her, and Melville seized the excuse to hurry below.

The first thing that struck him was that Red Feather's tomahawk and knife still lay in the corner where he had placed them. He simply held his rifle which most likely he was ready to use against his own people whenever the necessity arose.

"Well, Dot, you *have* found a prize," said her brother, following the chief, who was looking over her shoulder; "I had no idea that mother had left anything behind; there's enough for all."

She insisted that the others should partake while she waited, but neither would permit it. No matter how a-hungered either might have been, he enjoyed the sight of seeing her eat tenfold more than in partaking himself.

And you may be sure that Dot did ample justice to the rich find. Melville cut a thick slice for her, and spread the butter and jam on it, while a portion of the milk was poured into a cup.

I never heard of a little girl who could eat a piece of bread well covered with jam or preserves without failing to get most of it on her mouth. Dot Clarendon was no exception to the rule; and before she was through a goodly part of it, the sticky sweet stuff was on her cheeks and nose. When she looked up at the two who were watching her, the sight was so comical that Red Feather did that which I do not believe he had done a dozen times in all his life—he threw back his head and laughed loud. Melville caught the contagion and gave way to his mirth, which was increased by the naive remark of Dot that she couldn't see anything to laugh at.

"He threw back his head and laughed loud."

The appetite of the young queen having been satisfied, Melville insisted on Red Feather sharing what was left with him. The Sioux declined at first, but yielded, and the remaining bread and milk furnished them a grateful and nourishing repast. They did not use all, but saved enough to supply another meal for Dot, whose appetite was sure to make itself felt before many hours passed by.

Like most boys of his age in these later days, Melville Clarendon carried a watch, which showed that it was past three o'clock in the afternoon. This was considerably later than he supposed, and proved that in the rush of incidents time had passed faster than he had suspected.

"What shall I do?" asked the youth, turning to the chief.

"Go—up up," he replied, pointing up the steps; "watch out. Red Feather—he watch out here."

"Do you want Dot to stay with you?" asked Melville, pausing on his way to the steps.

"Leave wid Red Feather—he take heap care ob pappoose."

"There can be no doubt of *that*," remarked the brother, as he bounded up the stairs, resuming his former station near the window.

Looking out with the same care he had shown from the first, he found the Sioux had grown tired of galloping round the house and buildings, or they were plotting some other kind of mischief, for only one of them was in sight.

He was seated on his pony on the crest of the hill from which the signals were made to the Muddy Creek warriors. A moment's study of the red men showed that his attention was directed not toward the west but the north, in the direction of the settlement.

"He is now looking for enemies instead of friends," was the conclusion of Melville.

The truth was, the youth was beginning to wonder why the settlers did not come. If no accident had befallen his parents, they ought to have reached Barwell several hours before, and a gallop of ten miles was only a moderate ride for a party of horsemen eager to strike the marauders a blow.

But the fact that they were not yet in sight set the youth speculating as to what the result was likely to be if they did not come at all, or rather, if their coming should be delayed until nightfall, for it was not to be supposed that relief would not be sent sooner or later.

"There is only a faint moon to-night," he reflected; "and I'm afraid that's against us."

The American Indian prefers to do his mischief in the dark, and, since it would be impossible for the horsemen to conceal their approach, they would be likely to suffer in the first collision with the red men.

But, on the other hand, would not the gloom be of help to Red Feather in some scheme doubtless formed to help the children whose friend he had so suddenly become?

What the nature of this scheme was (if such existed) Melville could not guess; it might be that it required a bright moon for its success.

It may be said that the Sioux chieftain, as he stood beside one of the narrow windows on the lower floor, racked his brain until he hit upon a way of aiding the brother and sister—especially the latter—in their desperate peril. It was a strange plan, indeed, and, with all his adroitness, he knew the chances were ten to one against its success.

But the chief gave no hint to Melville of what was going on in his mind, and the latter could only wait, and hope and pray that the same Heavenly Father who had protected and preserved them thus far would keep them to the end.

The youth was in the midst of his speculations over the matter when he fancied he detected a peculiar odor from the outside. He could not tell its nature, though he snuffed the air repeatedly. He was alarmed, for he connected it with the silence of the war-party outside.

He was on the point of appealing to Red Feather downstairs, when its nature flashed upon him. *It was smoke!*

He had hardly reached the decision when a mass of thick vapor rolled in front of the house, so dense and blinding that for the moment it shut from his sight the mounted sentinel on the hill.

What was dreaded by the besieged had come at last. The Sioux, aware of the great value of the minutes, had resorted to the torch.

CHAPTER SEVEN

"A LITTLE CHILD SHALL LEAD THEM."— SURROUNDED BY PERIL

WITHIN a distance of a dozen yards of the house of Archibald Clarendon stood his barn. It was what might be called a nondescript building, being open at the bottom to an extent sufficient to admit his wagons, ploughs, farming implements, harnesses, and indeed about everything used in the cultivation of the fertile land.

In the upper portion were stowed his hay and grain, and in the rear of the lower part were the stables for his horses and cows. The latter, with his principal wagon, had been removed that morning, when the settler started with his family on their hasty flight northward to the settlement of Barwell; but the timber was dry, and enough hay was stored in the loft to render the building very combustible.

It was to this structure that the Sioux had applied the torch, and at the moment the smoke rolled in front of the house the whole building was in flames. Unfortunately, there was a gentle breeze blowing from the barn directly toward the house, and it was because of this favoring fact that the former was fired. The marauders had every reason to believe the flames would soon communicate with the dwelling and burn it to the ground.

The barn faced the end with the broad stone chimney, through which Red Feather made his singular entrance. It was therefore out of the field of vision of the inmates, since there was not a single window up or down stairs with an outlook in that direction.

Melville started to run down the steps on making the startling discovery, but met Red Feather coming up with one hand grasping that of Dot.

"My gracious!" exclaimed the youth; "what can be done now, Red Feather? We shall all be burned alive."

"Oogh! not yet—house ain't afire!" replied the chieftain, without any evidence of excitement.

"But the wind is blowing this way, and the house is sure to go."

"Mebbe go—mebbe won't go," was the reply with the same stolidity of manner; "wait—see bimeby."

It would seem that, since the Sioux had such a good chance to do mischief, they would have applied the fire to the house itself. But, though the logs were dry enough to burn readily when the flames were fairly started, it was still a task requiring considerable time and work. It was necessary to pile the fuel against the logs, and to nurse the flames until they set the heavy material going. The barn was so inflammable that a tiny match would ignite it, and, should the fire reach the house, the task would be equally effective, and far more enjoyable to the cruel spectators.

"It was to this structure that the Sioux had applied the torch."

While Red Feather and Melville stood near each other on the upper floor, talking in low tones, Dot slipped her hand from the grasp of the chieftain, and walking to the side of the bed on which she had been lying, knelt down, closed her eyes, and clasped her hands, just as she had been accustomed to do at her mother's knee ever since she was old enough to form the words after her parent.

"She is praying," whispered her brother.

After repeating a simple prayer for their safety the child opened her eyes, and, seeing her friends looking at her, she sprang nimbly up and ran to them.

"Don't be scared, brother and Red Feather; I prayed that we might all be taken care of, and I'm not afraid one bit now, are you?"

Melville tried to speak, but his voice choked him. His eyes filled, and, lifting the precious one in his arms, he pressed her to his breast and kissed her again and again.

The chieftain said nothing, but he too raised the child in his arms and touched his lips to hers. Not only that, but he filled her with delight by saluting Susie in the same manner.

Who shall try to make known the emotions which stirred that savage heart? He had often turned in scorn from the words of the good missionaries who had come to his country; but there was something in the faith of the sweet child which touched his nature as it had never been touched before.

Having set the little one on her feet, the Sioux stepped across the main room to the window from which most of their observations had been made on that floor. Melville followed him, and noticed that the smoke had vanished, so that the sentinel on the hill was in sight again.

Red Feather thrust his hand through the windows, so that his fingers projected slightly beyond. This was done to ascertain the direction of the wind.

"Oogh!" he muttered, with a curious expression on his countenance "*wind blow oder way!* Great Spirit hear what pappoose say."

"Can it be possible?" asked the awed Melville.

There was no doubt of it; the slight breeze, which had been coming directly from the barn toward the house had changed, and was now blowing in exactly the opposite direction.

The chief and the youth passed into the smaller apartment which was nearest the chimney. The former pressed his ear against the logs to help his hearing. Had they caught the flames from the barn, which was still burning furiously, he could not have failed to detect the fact. A moment's attention told him that up to the present the building was safe.

But it was not in the nature of things that the Sioux should refrain because their first effort failed. They were not the ones to give up on a single trial.

Several noteworthy things took place during the latter part of this eventful afternoon. First of all, there was such a decided lowering of the temperature that a fire would have felt comfortable to the occupants of the building. It looked indeed to Melville as though one of those fearful storms known in the west as "blizzards" was approaching.

This was hardly possible, for it was summer-time, but the plains of Texas and many portions of the west are often swept by what are termed "northers" during the warm season. These winds are accompanied by such cutting cold that people and animals often perish, the suddenness of the visitation shutting them out from securing refuge.

Red Feather offered his blanket to Dot, but she shook her head. "It's too dirty," she said, noticing the soot which the owner did not seem to mind; "I can use a blanket from the bed, for mamma did not take them all with her."

Had Melville suspected the thought in the mind of his little sister, he would have checked its utterance through fear of offending the chieftain, but there was no need of that: one of the impossibilities was for Dot to hurt his feelings.

The next most interesting event was the second failure of the Sioux to set fire to the house. This was singular, for there seemed no reason why they should not have succeeded with such facilities at command.

The barn burned so readily that long before dusk it was reduced to a mass of smoking ruins.

From these, it would have appeared, enough brands could have been collected to make a bonfire of the structure.

Several of the Sioux gathered fuel at one corner of the building, and made an attempt to fire it. The sounds which reached those within left no doubt of what was going on, and you may be sure they listened with anxiety.

It was while matters were in this critical shape that Melville put the direct question to Red Feather as to what he would do in the event of the house being fired. The chieftain replied that, when he saw there was no saving the building, he intended to take Dot in his arms and walk out of the door among his own warriors. The lad was to follow immediately, and he would insist that the lives of the children should be spared because of the promise made by him to them.

Pressed further, the chief admitted that the plan was likely to be only partially successful. He was confident he could save Dot, because of her sex and years; but there was little hope for Melville. Unless prevented by the care of the little girl, Red Feather was willing to join in the fight which the youth would have to make for his life with scarcely an earthly prospect of winning.

But the attempt to fire the log structure came to naught, and, strangest of all, the Sioux gave it up—at least for a time, for it would have been contrary to Indian nature had they abandoned the effort to destroy their enemies so long as there was a chance of success.

Thus matters stood until the shadows of night began closing over the prairie. During the interval, many glimpses of the Sioux had been caught, as they moved backward and forward at will, sometimes mounted and often on foot. The sentinel kept his place on the crest of the hill, or rather, he exchanged it with one of his brother warriors, who walked about, sat down, smoked his pipe, and used every means at his command to cause the time to pass comfortably to him.

The failure of the arrival of help caused not only surprise but distress to Melville Clarendon; for there was but one way of interpreting it: something had befallen his parents by which they were prevented from reaching the settlement.

The youth had tried all through the afternoon to drive away the misgivings which had troubled him on this score; but he could do so no longer. It was in keeping with the tactics of the Indians that, after arranging to attack the home of Clarendons, they should circle to the northward, so as to approach it from the direction of the settlement. Had they done this, with a view of shutting off all escape to Barwell, it was more than likely they did it early enough in the day to meet the pioneer and his wife hurrying from the place of danger.

Had this meeting taken place, nothing could have saved the couple. Melville secured some consolation from the belief that, if such an awful calamity had overtaken his parents, the Sioux would give evidence of the fact. That is to say, they would have taken possession of the horses and enough of the property for the lad to see them on the first survey of the assailants.

The fact that he did not detect anything of the kind might be accepted as proof that no meeting had taken place with the particular party under the leadership of Red Feather.

But that question was easily answered by Red Feather himself. He assured Melville that he and his warriors had come from the south, arriving on the spot only a short time before the appearance of the brother and sister on the other bank of the stream. He had waved his blanket at the children as a taunt, not supposing they would come any closer after seeing him; but, riding over the hill, he peeped cautiously back, and learned that Melville, not catching the meaning of the gesture, was approaching his home. Thereupon the chief called back his men who were riding off, and arranged to secure the young birds returning to the nest from which the parents had flown.

All the comfort that the youth might have got from this story was spoiled by the declaration of the chief that he believed an encounter had taken place between Mr. Clarendon and the other party of Sioux which reached the spot later in the afternoon. These were under the lead of Tall Bear, a rival of Red Feather, between whom a jealousy amounting to bitter enmity existed.

Had Red Feather not seen Tall Bear among the group he would have adopted a course which the presence of that rival prevented. He would have gone out among his own warriors, and insisted on his rights with a vigor that could hardly have failed of success. Though his men were not afraid of dispute with him, yet they were not likely to invite violence. When they saw he was fully resolved they would yield. The conclusion to be reached from this statement is that Red Feather after all did not make half as determined an argument in behalf of his friends as he appeared to have done. Melville, therefore, was right in his first suspicion, though he was too thoughtful to say so.

"Something unusual was going on among the Sioux outside."

Darkness had not fully come when it became clear to the watchers within the building that something unusual was going on among the Sioux outside. Nearly the entire party came together on the crest of the hill, where they were only dimly visible in the gathering gloom. They could be seen walking back and forth, making many gestures, and talking so loud that their voices were clearly heard.

"Red Feather strained his hearing to catch some words."

Leaning against the side of the window, Red Feather strained his hearing to catch some words that would give him an inkling of what it all meant.

The heart of the youth throbbed with the hope that the long-expected help was in sight at last. It seemed to him the Sioux were acting just as they would do in case they detected the approach of hostile horsemen.

But the sorely-tried lad could only wait until Red Feather should answer the question on his tongue, or until it should be answered by the events themselves.

CHAPTER EIGHT

TALL BEAR AND HIS WARRIORS—A SURPRISING DISCOVERY

YOU will recall that when Red Feather wedged himself in the narrow window he said, in answer to the sharp questioning of Melville Clarendon, that the Muddy Creek band of Sioux were so far off that nothing was to be feared from them.

The original band of marauders numbered over a score, and were under the joint leadership of Tall Bear and Red Feather, both of whom were eager to sweep along the thin line of settlements like a cyclone, scattering death and destruction in their path. It may strike you that so small a force was hardly equal to the task of such a raid; but I have only to remind you that the famous Geronimo and his Apaches, who made their home among the alkali deserts and mountain fastnesses of Arizona and New Mexico, numbered few warriors at times, and yet they baffled for years a regiment of United States cavalry. It was only when the chieftain chose to come in and surrender himself under the pledge of good treatment that hostilities ended.

The twenty-odd horsemen under the leadership of Red Feather and Tall Bear were fitting types of that savage horde which in the early summer of 1876 blotted out General Custer and his troops. It so happened, however, with the smaller party that they found no such favoring circumstances to help them. At the first settler's cabin assailed they discovered the inmates ready for them. In some way or other, several families had learned of their danger in time to prepare for their assailants.

It was clear to the Indians that the settlers in that section had taken the alarm, and Red Feather proposed they should abandon their first plan and push northward towards Barwell, attacking the isolated homes to the south of that settlement. Tall Bear opposed so warmly, and with such slurs on his rival, that a personal conflict was narrowly averted.

The end of the quarrel was that Red Feather, with five of his followers, drew off from the rest and rode northward. The result of this separation was unsatisfactory to both parties.

The friendly Indian who had hastened toward Barwell to warn the pioneers of their danger did his work so well that hardly one was neglected. The inmates of the first cabin attacked by Red Feather were awaiting him.

Only a few shots were exchanged, when the wrathful chieftain withdrew, and, pushing to the northward, next swooped down on the dwelling of Archibald Clarendon.

No resistance was encountered there, for, as you know, the inmates had left some time before. For some reason never fully explained, Red Feather did not fire the buildings at once. Shortly after, Melville Clarendon and his sister appeared on the scene, and the incidents which followed have already been told.

Meanwhile, Tall Bear and his warriors met with no better success than the smaller party. The proof became so strong that the whole district was on the alert that he abruptly changed his mind and led his warriors at a sweeping gallop to the northward over the trail of Red Feather and his warriors.

When he arrived on the scene he heard the curious story the five warriors had to tell. A dwelling at last had been found in which the occupants were not fully prepared, or rather, were so insignificant in strength that no company of Sioux, however small, could consent to a repulse.

But there stood the cabin defying them. Red Feather had forced his way partly through the window and then was caught so fast that, but for the mercy of the sturdy youth within, he would have been killed without being able to use a finger to defend himself.

Among the whole party who heard the remarkable narrative, there was not one who would have thought of keeping a promise made under such circumstances as was that of the chief. No pledge could have been more solemn, and yet those are the very ones that are first repudiated by the red man.

To Tall Bear and his band the action of Red Feather in descending the chimney was natural. The bitterest enemy of the chieftain never questioned his courage, and, knowing how chagrined he must feel over his mishap, they could understand the desperate feeling that prompted the deed, the like of which was seldom if ever known before.

There was little said about Red Feather's wish to keep his agreement with Melville, for the reason I have already hinted—his proposal to do so was not earnest enough to mislead them.

But to the Sioux outside it looked very much as if the descent of the chimney by the chief had marked the end of his career. Among all the warriors there was not one who believed the truth—that he had been

- 57 -

changed from the fiercest enemy into the most beloved friend of the boy and girl.

The tantalizing shout of Melville from the window was proof to the warriors that Red Feather had been slain by the boy, though, as I have said, no report of a gun was heard from within the building.

The chieftain's course, after proving himself a friend of the brother and sister, showed his desire to keep his presence in the house unsuspected by his own people. He took care that no glimpse of him was caught through the windows, and he refrained from firing when he had any number of chances to bring down an Indian.

Doubtless there were several reasons for this forbearance. Such a shot would be credited to Melville, and might excite the Sioux to an attack too furious to be resisted. At the same time, it is hardly to be supposed that Red Feather's feelings had so changed, because of his wish to save Dot and her brother, that he was ready to turn about and begin shooting at the very ones whom he had led on this raid.

It cannot be said that Tall Bear grieved any more over the loss of his rival leader than did most of the warriors. He prudently uttered some words of sympathy, but they hardly deceived those who heard them. They agreed with him, however, in declaring that his fall must be avenged, and that the boy who had caused his death, as well as his little sister, must suffer torture-punishment for the deed.

Several circuits around the building proved that it could hardly be carried by the most determined assault in their power. All the windows were too narrow to be used as a means of entrance, even if any one was brave enough to repeat the disastrous experiment of the other chief. The single door had already resisted the strongest shock they could give it, and no weak point was visible.

True, the path used by Red Feather when he finally succeeded in gaining the interior was open to the rest; but it is no reflection on their courage to say that among the whole party there was not one willing to head the procession down the chimney, even though but a solitary boy and a single rifle stood in the way.

Clearly there was one means at the command of Tall Bear and his Sioux which was not only terrible, but effective. They could set fire to the building and reduce it to ashes.

The lookout on the hill reported the horizon clear in every direction; and, since his wide sweep of vision extended toward every point of the compass, he was able to discover the approach of hostile horsemen a good while before they could reach the spot. He knew that if help came it would be from the northward, where Barwell lay, whither Mr. Clarendon and his wife had hurried on the first alarm. The prairie for a couple of miles was under a scrutiny that would let nothing escape.

The circumstances were so favorable that Tall Bear and his party decided to indulge in a feast. Enough poultry were wandering about the premises to afford a fine meal for a larger band than he had with him, and it took only a short time to wring the necks of more than a score of ducks and chickens.

The Sioux gathered to the westward of the barn and ate like so many wild animals until all were satisfied. The meal finished, they gave their attention to the serious business before them. Had the incidents I am relating taken place half a century ago, the red men would have been obliged to resort to the old-fashioned flint and steel with which our forefathers used to start a fire; but they were abreast of these modern times to that extent that nearly every one carried more or less lucifer-matches.

The favoring wind led to the barn being fired, under the belief that the flames would quickly communicate with the house but a short distance off; but, as you have learned, Providence favored the threatened ones to that extent that the breeze changed its course, and for a time Dot and Melville were saved.

"His attention was drawn to the sentinel on the hill."

Tall Bear and the Sioux waited till, to their disappointment and surprise, they saw the barn sink into blazing ruins and leave the house intact.

The next proceeding was to gather what embers they could and pile them against the dwelling, where they speedily burst into flames. It now looked certain that the structure was doomed; but the heavy logs, although dry on the outside, were damp within. It takes such timber a long time to part with its natural moisture, and, fortunately for our friends, a driving rain-storm less than a week previous had so soaked the wood that only an intense and long-continued heat could set it aflame. The logs were charred and scorched, and more than once appeared to be on the point of breaking into a roaring blaze; but the brands piled against the end of the house finally sank down to embers and ashes, and though considerable smoke arose, the house stood really as firm and as strong as at the first.

This was a keener disappointment than Tall Bear had yet met, for it looked as though the most potent if not the only means at his command was powerless to bring the boy to terms.

The chieftain himself examined the logs which had been subjected to the fire. He dug his hunting-knife into them, and soon discovered why they resisted the fire so effectually. Then he tested other parts of the house in the same manner and with the same result.

For the first time since his arrival on the spot he was forced to see the probability of another failure. His career from the hour he bounded upon his pony and entered so eagerly on the raid had been a continual disappointment. He was angered and resentful toward the supposed dead Red Feather, because he allowed himself to be baffled at the beginning by a solitary boy.

Tall Bear's pride was stirred, and he was unwilling to confess himself beaten after openly blaming his predecessor for failing to capture the place with less than one-third of his force.

But there seemed to be no help for it, unless he should persevere with the fire until the logs of the house were forced into combustion. They must yield in time, if the effort was kept up; and he was on the point of renewing the attempt on a larger scale than before when his attention was drawn to the sentinel on the hill, who uttered the startling cry that horsemen were in sight to the northward.

"More Sioux comin'—open door quick."

The chief and the warriors who were not already on the spot hurried thither to learn what it meant.

As I have explained elsewhere, this discovery did not take place until near nightfall, when darkness was beginning to render surrounding objects indistinct. The long delay in the arrival of help for the children of the pioneer led Tall Bear to believe it was not likely to come before morning; but once more it looked as if Providence was about to interfere to bring his wicked schemes to naught.

The gloom overspreading stream and prairie prevented the Sioux from seeing the horsemen clearly enough to identify them. The forms were so shadowy and vague that nothing more could be learned than that there were about a dozen men mounted on horses, and riding toward the cabin on a slow walk, as if not without some misgiving.

It was certain that while the sentinel on the hill commanded an unusually wide sweep of vision, he himself was conspicuous, and the others had been as quick to discover him as he was to detect them. Both parties, therefore, were aware of the presence of the other, and neither was likely to make a mistake at this critical juncture.

But neither Tall Bear nor any of his warriors could tell of a surety whether the approaching horsemen were white or red men. The Sioux grouped around the house were not the only ones by any means that were engaged on this memorable raid in Southern Minnesota, and it was not impossible that a party of friends were in sight.

It was somewhat curious that the majority of the Sioux believed a party of their own people at hand. Tall Bear himself was inclined to think the same; but to guard against any fatal mistake, he directed his warriors to ride down the hill on the east, so as to interpose between them and the strangers, who could now be barely distinguished.

Two other Sioux were to wait until the horsemen came near enough to settle the question, when they would make it known by signal, after which the course of the band would be open. If the new-comers proved to be enemies, a sharp fight was likely to follow, in which serious damage was certain to be inflicted on both sides.

The directions of the leader were promptly followed, the warriors galloping off and quickly disappearing in the direction of the upper trail, along which Melville and Dot had ridden on their way from the settlement.

"The door swung inward."

While they were thus engaged, Tall Bear cantered to the front of the cabin and leaped to the ground. He had determined to attempt a trick.

Striking his fist against the door, he called out—

"More Sioux comin'—open door quick—Tall Bear won't hurt—don't wait."

He hoped the actions of himself and warriors had made known the former fact before he announced it in words. He counted upon a panic that would show the lad his situation was hopeless, and induce him to surrender while there was hope of mercy.

There was no reply to his summons, and he raised his fist to strike the door again, when he discovered the latch-string on the outside. With no suspicion of what it meant, he gave it a twitch.

To his amazement, the door swung inward of its own weight, and, before he could check himself, he had to take a step within to escape falling.

With a vague suspicion of the truth, he called to the lad again, and groped about the lower room.

He quickly discovered that it was empty, and then, with little personal fear, he hurried up the stairs.

Two minutes were enough to make clear the truth.

He was the only living person in the cabin!

CHAPTER NINE

NAT TRUMBULL AND HIS MEN—OUT IN THE NIGHT

THE American Indian rarely shows any emotion that may be stirring his heart. I am sure, however, that if one could have had a look at the face of Tall Bear when he made the discovery that neither the brother nor sister was in the cabin he would have seen a picture of as blank amazement as ever held a person speechless.

This was not caused so much by what the children had done as by the course of the Sioux themselves, for nothing was plainer to the chieftain than the manner in which Melville and Dot had escaped.

They had been on the alert, and when the warriors hastened to the top of the hill Melville Clarendon was bright enough to seize the opportunity thus given. He had quietly stepped out of the front door, where, in the gloom and the absorbing interest of the red men in another direction, neither he nor the little girl attracted notice. The two were doubtless making all haste from the endangered spot.

But the chieftain was astounded over another discovery: in order to make his search absolutely thorough he had caught up a smouldering brand, quickly fanned it into a flame, and then explored the upper and lower storys. Not a nook or corner was left unvisited, and a hiding cat would have been brought to light.

That which almost knocked Tall Bear breathless was the fact that he found nothing of the remains of Red Feather, who had entered the chimney before the eyes of five of his own warriors.

"Explored the upper and lower storys."

The inference was certain: Red Feather had not been killed, but had gone out of the front door just as the children had done.

Tall Bear was still far from suspecting the whole truth, though, had he been left with nothing else on his mind for a short time only, he must have divined, or at least suspected, what actually took place.

But a party of horsemen were approaching, and must already be close at hand. They required attention, for if they should prove to be enemies, the chief would have his hands full. His position, with a lighted torch within the building, was not the most prudent he could take, and as he came outside he flung the light to the ground where it sputtered out in the darkness.

Tall Bear's pony was standing where he had left him, and vaulting lightly upon his back, he sent him on a gallop to the top of the hill, to learn something about the new-comers.

The main party of warriors were some distance off, awaiting the signal to know whether they were to fight or to join the parties whose identity was still in doubt. The couple whom Tall Bear had despatched to reconnoitre were still absent, so that he found himself alone on the elevation.

It is at such times that the American Indian displays a wonderful keenness of sight and hearing. The chief sat motionless, peering into the gloom and listening. None could know better than he that he had taken a most dangerous position.

If the horsemen, who could not be far off, were hostile, they would surround the hill whereon they last saw the Sioux, and unless Tall Bear kept his wits about him he was likely to be shut in on every hand.

But it would have been hard for the most skilful Indian scout to take him unawares. He was certain to see and hear the approach of any one as soon as the latter could see or hear him, and the chieftain was not the one to fall asleep under such circumstances.

Darting his penetrating glances here, there, and everywhere, he suddenly fixed them upon a point directly ahead. Something was vaguely assuming form in the gloom, and a minute later he observed a man walking toward him.

Tall Bear leaned forward over the neck of his pony, that he might not lose the advantage of an inch of space. The stranger was advancing without any more noise than if he was a shadow, and he was alone, or, if he had any companions, they were so far behind when he was in full view as to be invisible.

The man on foot came to a halt while still too far off to be more than faintly visible, and emitted a low tremulous whistle. Tall Bear promptly answered in the same manner, and then the other ran forward to his side. He was one of the two scouts the chief had sent out, and he brought important tidings.

The party of horsemen which caused the Sioux such concern were white men—every one—under the leadership of the famous frontier scout Nat Trumbull. The warrior had ventured near enough to the company to recognize his voice when he gave the order for his men to move around to the south and approach the house from that direction.

Trumbull was a veteran who had done good service during the lurid summer of 1862, when the Sioux desolated a large portion of the Minnesota frontier, and Tall Bear feared him more than any white man living. He knew that if Trumbull and his rangers got a chance at the Sioux they would force matters without mercy. No sooner, therefore, did the Sioux scout tell what he had learned than Tall Bear made up his mind that the best place for him and his warriors was somewhere else. When he asked after the other scout who accompanied the one that returned, the chieftain was told that he had ventured so near the white men that he narrowly escaped capture, and was forced to dodge off in another direction.

That was enough. Tall Bear wheeled his pony like a flash, and galloped toward the point where he knew his warriors were awaiting the news with as much anxiety as his own.

Such tidings travel fast, and within five minutes after the return of the scout with his message Tall Bear and his warriors were riding as if for life from the neighborhood.

It may as well be explained how it was that the relief which Melville Clarendon expected hours before was so delayed that, but for an unexpected occurrence, it would have arrived too late.

You have learned that Mr. Clarendon and his wife left their home early that morning and hurried northward over the ten miles between them and Barwell.

All went well until they had passed half the distance, when the sudden appearance of three mounted Indians showed that they were not likely to get through without trouble. The settler at once came to a halt and prepared to make the best defence possible. The animals were gathered near the wagon, where Mr. Clarendon made his wife crouch down to escape the flying bullets, and, loaded gun in hand, he waited the attack that was sure to come.

A skilful marksman in the situation of Mr. Clarendon generally considers himself the equal of three mounted men on the open plain, and the conduct of the warriors showed that they held the settler in respect. Keeping beyond easy range, they circled about the wagon and its inmates as if looking for an opening, and finally all three brought their guns to their shoulders and let fly.

The volley killed one of the horses, which dropped dead as he stood near the wagon.

The settler instantly returned the shot, and—rather curiously—though the distance was considerable, he brought down the pony of the nearest Indian, which made such a frenzied leap that his rider was thrown. Mr. Clarendon at first thought it was he who had been struck; but he quickly sprang to his feet and vaulted upon another pony behind one of his comrades.

The Sioux continued circling around the settler at a still greater distance, and sent in another volley, which did no harm. At last they concluded the risk of a charge and attack too great, and drew off, finally disappearing in the distance.

"He brought down the pony of the nearest Indian."

Mr. Clarendon waited an hour or more, expecting them to return, but they did not, and he resumed his journey to the settlement.

Having but a single horse, he was obliged to leave part of his load behind, and such slow progress was made in his crippled condition that the day was well gone before he reached Barwell.

There he was startled to learn that his children had started homeward early in the day, and were still absent. He set about organizing a rescue party at once. Fortunately, Nat Trumbull and several of his rangers were present, and they eagerly gave their help. Within half an hour after the father received the alarming tidings Trumbull was cantering southward with a dozen tried men and true, and among them was Archibald Clarendon himself.

Although the escape of the three parties from the beleaguered cabin may strike you as wonderful, yet, after all, there was nothing very remarkable in it.

Red Feather would have forgotten his lifelong training, had he failed to see and take instant advantage of the providential diversion when the Sioux, in the gathering darkness, made all haste to the top of the hill to learn about the horsemen approaching from the north.

Had the Sioux suspected that the brain of one of their shrewdest chiefs was helping the boy and girl, they would have been far more vigilant; but, as it was, they must have believed that nothing could draw the lad outside of his shelter until the appearance of his friends.

Red Feather was standing as before at one of the upper windows when the stampede took place to the crest of the hill. He read its meaning, and saw his golden opportunity.

"Now we go," he said in an undertone; "me carry pappoose (child)—you come 'long—put blanket round—den look like Indian."

There was another reason for using the blanket; the air was cold enough to require it.

Melville was quick to catch the idea, and, whipping a quilt from the bed, he gathered it about his shoulders, so that it came almost to his crown. His straw hat would have been too conspicuous, and he held that in front of his breast, under the blanket, to be put in its proper place again when it should become safe to do so.

"I'm ready," he said, standing erect, and looking at Red Feather as well as he could in the gloom.

"Me too."

The chief had lifted Dot in his arms, and he covered her with his thick blanket, doing so with such skill that hardly any one would have suspected the nature of the precious burden he carried next to his heart.

Not a minute was lost. Red Feather passed down the steps, paused in front of the door, and waited for Melville to unfasten it. The youth donned his hat, flung aside his blanket, and set his gun down to give his arms play. The heavy bar was lifted from its place, and then, in obedience to an odd whim, he thrust the end of the leathern string through the orifice above the latch.

He gathered his blanket about his shoulders and head as before, doffing his hat and returning it to its hiding-place, and paused for the chieftain to precede him.

Red Feather stood a minute on the threshold, peering out in the darkness. Everything looked favorable, and he stepped forward. Melville was directly behind him, and softly closed the door as he left the cabin.

The Sioux, instead of walking straight away from the building, moved stealthily along the front, passed around the corner, and started southward. By this means he interposed the cabin between himself and the party on the hill.

- 69 -

"The youth was almost on his heels. His heart beat fast, and he was eager to break into a run."

The youth was almost on his heels. His heart beat fast, and he was eager to break into a run that would quickly increase the distance between him and the war-party. He was about to suggest that they should hasten, when, to his surprise, he perceived that his friend was moving so much faster than he that he threatened to leave him out of sight altogether. Red Feather had struck a peculiar gait. It looked as if he was walking, but his pace was a loping trot, in which the feet were lifted only slightly from the ground. The movement was as smooth as that of a pacing horse, and he adopted it in order to save Dot from jolting.

The Sioux, on emerging from the building, had glanced sharply about him, in the hope of catching sight of his own pony, or one belonging to a warrior; but there was none convenient, and he dared not wait.

"Saladin must be hovering somewhere in the neighborhood," thought his young owner, "and it would be mighty fine if I could run against him, but it doesn't look as if there is much chance."

Red Feather continued his loping gait for two or three hundred yards, when he once more dropped to a walk; but his steps were so lengthy and rapid that the lad had to trot most of the time to hold his own.

Melville fancied his leader was changing his course, but he could only guess its direction. Looking back, nothing was visible of the cabin left a few minutes before. Everything was dark, the country being an undulating prairie. Mr. Clarendon used no fences, and the ground travelled by the fugitives had not been broken.

It seemed to the youth that the most natural thing for Red Feather to do was to make directly for the settlement, ten miles to the northward. It was a long tramp, but the two were capable of doing much more without special fatigue.

The chieftain did not speak as he hurried forward; and the boy asked him no questions, content to wait until he chose to tell his plans. His pace grew more moderate, and soon became easy for Melville to keep his place beside him.

It need not be said that both made good use of their eyes and ears. Although beyond sight of the house, it was too soon to think themselves safe. If a collision took place between Tall Bear and the new-comers, some of the Indians were likely to be skurrying backwards and forwards on their ponies, and it was probable they would come upon the fugitives.

Whenever Red Feather should meet his fellows there would be a sensation, but he was not the warrior to shrink the test, though he wished it to be deferred until the brother and sister were beyond the resentment of every one of his tribe.

CHAPTER TEN

AN OLD FRIEND—SEPARATED

SUDDENLY Red Feather stopped. Melville did the same, wondering what the cause could be.

The youth stood so near that he saw the chief was looking to the right, as though he had heard a suspicious sound or saw something in that direction. The lad gave close attention, since he could detect nothing.

The Indian resumed his walk more slowly than before, but did not utter a word. His glances, however, to one side showed he was not free from misgiving, and by-and-by he stopped walking and listened intently as before.

"What is it?" asked Melville, giving way to his curiosity.

"Me hear something," was the reply, the Indian going still slower.

"I can't detect anything," said the lad, as though the fact ought to lighten the fears of the other.

Red Feather now tenderly placed Dot on her feet. The little one was half asleep, and rubbed her eyes after the manner of children when disturbed.

A whispered word from her brother kept her quiet, and, kneeling down, Red Feather pressed his ear to the ground, holding it there for a full minute. Then he raised his head a few inches, looked off into the darkness, placed the side of his face against the ground for a few seconds more, after which he rose to his feet.

Instead of explaining, he turned to Melville.

"You see Red Feather do—you do same as him."

Melville promptly obeyed, assuming the same posture that his friend had taken. Closing his eyes, so as to shut out everything that might distract his senses, he gave all his efforts to that of hearing.

Yes, he *did* hear something—just the faintest irregular beating on the ground—so faint indeed that he would not have believed it anything except for what the Sioux had said.

"Hear nuffin?" asked the other, as the boy came to his feet.

"Yes, I think I did hear a faint noise."

"What him be?"

"That's more than I can tell, Red Feather."

"Hoss—hear hoss walking—dat what hear."

"Is that the fact?" asked Melville, somewhat startled, peering toward the same point of the compass at which the chief had gazed though the lad had no other idea of the right course.

"Hoss—he come dis way."

"If that is so there is likely to be someone on him, and I don't think it is well for us to meet him."

To this wise remark Red Feather gave no answer, but continued peering in the same direction as before.

"If there is one horseman there is likely to be more———"

Melville cut short his own words, and whistled cautiously, checking that with equal suddenness, through fear of offending his friend.

But the chief showed no displeasure, and, before anything could be said, the form of a riderless horse came out of the gloom and trotted forward with a faint neigh of pleasure.

"Saladin, my own Saladin!" exclaimed the delighted youth, flinging his arms around the outstretched neck, and actually touching his lips to the silken nose of the noble steed.

"Saladin, old fellow, I'm proud of you," said Melville; "the Sioux did their best to steal you away from us, but you were too smart for them. One was cruel enough to shoot at you, but it don't look as if he did any damage."

The youth could not resist the temptation to place his foot in the stirrup, and leap into the saddle, where he was "at home."

"Now, Red Feather," he added, "things are beginning to look up; I can relieve you of carrying Dot; the truth is that after we cross the stream I shall feel safe. Under heaven, we owe everything to you; but you need go no farther with us."

"Ain't safe," said the chieftain sententiously; "Injins all round—Red Feather go all way home wid pappoose."

"That is very kind, but I can relieve you of your burden."

"Me carry pappoose," replied the Sioux, moving toward the little one.

"Dot," said her brother, "which would you rather do—ride on Saladin with me or let Red Feather carry you?"

"A riderless horse came out of the gloom."

"It's a good deal nicer to have him carry me; take me, Red Feather," she added, reaching out her arms.

Melville was glad to hear this answer, for he knew it would touch the chieftain, whose heart had become wrapped up in the sweet little one.

Before he could lift her, however, he paused, and, saying "Wait," again knelt down with his ear to the ground.

The result was satisfactory, and, remarking that he heard nothing more, he stood upon his feet, stooped over, and lifted the little one to her old place. Then the flight was taken up as before.

Melville held Saladin back, so as to follow the leader, who reached the side of the stream a few minutes later. Objects were indistinct, but the youth was so familiar with the spot that he recognized it as the Upper Crossing. When the lad would have lost himself the Sioux had gone as unerringly to the spot as though the sun were shining overhead to guide him.

"Now," said Melville, as they waited a minute or two on the brink, "there is no need for you to wade across, and wet your leggings to the knees; it can be easily fixed."

"Oogh! heap big load for hoss—carry all."

The lad laughed.

"That isn't what I mean; the pony is strong enough to bear us, but it isn't necessary; I'll ride him over, and then send him back after you."

This was a sensible course, for, though an Indian cares little for the inconvenience of wading through water of considerable depth, yet he will not do so when there in any practicable means of avoiding it.

"You must be careful," added Melville, as he was about to ride into the current, "for there are some deep places which the horse will have to skirt closely. If he steps into one, he will go over his depth, and that will make it bad for you and Dot; I think I had better carry her over with me."

"Oogh! Red Feather know holes, 'cause he fall in 'em—mebbe you fall in wid pappoose—how den, eh?"

"All right," replied the youth with a smile, as he gave the word to Saladin, who began wading with the same snuffing and care that his kind always show when entering a body of water.

His rider was wise enough to decide that the safest course was to leave everything to him, for he had travelled that way often enough to be familiar with its dangers.

He narrowly missed plunging into a hole near the other bank, but he saved himself, and finally emerged on the farther shore with his rider dry-shod.

"Now, old fellow," said Melville, affectionately patting his head, "go back and bring over Red Feather and Dot. Try not to come as near making a slip as you did with me."

"Go back and bring over Red Feather and Dot."

The pony showed his comprehension of the request by stepping at once in the stream and making his way toward the other shore.

Long before the little party reached the stream just crossed by Melville night had fully come. The moon did not rise until late in the evening, and the darkness was such that, after parting with Saladin, he saw him vanish when he was no more than half-way across the creek. Of course, therefore, Red Feather and Dot were out of sight altogether.

Melville sat down on the sloping bank, with his rifle across his knees, to await the coming of his friend. In the stillness, the slightest sound could be heard a long way. The plashing of the pony's feet as he carefully felt his way through the water was so plain that it was easy to tell every step he took.

The youth was looking idly off in the gloom when he observed a rapidly growing light toward the south-east, which you will bear in mind was on the other side of the stream. He watched it for a minute or two, when the cause became apparent.

A couple of miles east of the Clarendon home was that of the nearest neighbor. He was without any family, his only companion being a hired man. They had received warning of the impending danger in time to escape, but being well mounted and armed, took a different direction from that leading toward Barwell, whither Mr. Clarendon and his wife hastened.

They were gone, but their property remained. The buildings were more extensive than those of Mr. Clarendon, and they had been fired by the Sioux. They created a huge glare which lit up the horizon in every direction.

"It must be," thought Melville, "that Tall Bear and his warriors have been scared away by the appearance of white men, and have touched off those buildings out of revenge. If Red Feather and I could have only known that friends were coming we could have stayed at home. I wonder they didn't try to fire that again, now that they can get inside and have so much better chance."

Melville watched the glare growing brighter and brighter, until it suddenly occurred to him that Red Feather was a long time in crossing the stream. The light from the conflagration brought the opposite shore into faint view, but failed to reveal the Sioux. While the youth was looking and wondering, however, he heard the splashing of water and observed Saladin making his way back.

But, instead of doing so at the regular ferry-place, he had gone some distance above, where the depth was greater. Even while staring at the pony, the animal sank down so low that it was plain he was swimming.

This of itself was curious, without the additional fact that there was no one upon his back; he was returning, as may be said, empty handed.

As you may well believe, Melville was startled and alarmed; something unusual must have happened on the other shore. There could be no doubt that Saladin had gone entirely across, and now came back without the chief who expected to ride over the ford.

The lad rose and walked down to the edge of the water to meet his steed. The latter was obliged to swim only a short distance, when the depth became so shallow that his body rose above the surface, and he quickly stepped out on dry land.

"What can this mean?" muttered Melville examining the wetted saddle, bridle, and accoutrements; "were you sent back, Saladin, or did you come of your own accord? Ah, if you had the gift of speech!"

It seemed to the lad that he could discern something moving on the other side, but, with the help of the glare of the distant fire, he could not make it out.

He ventured to signal to Red Feather by means of the whistle with which he was accustomed to summon Saladin. The Sioux was sure to identify it if it reached his ears.

The signal was emitted with such care that it could not have been heard more than a hundred yards away, and the youth listened with a rapidly beating heart for the reply.

It came, but in a far different form than was expected or desired. The sounds showed that other animals had entered the water and were approaching the opposite bank. At this juncture, too, the glare from the burning buildings increased to that extent that the other shore came out more distinctly than ever.

To his dismay Melville observed that the bank was lined with mounted Indians, three of whom had already ridden into the stream and were urging their ponies across. They were doing this, too, with a skill which left no doubt that they knew all about the holes into which one was likely to plunge.

Where these Sioux—as they undoubtedly were—could have come from with such abruptness was more than the startled lad could tell, though he naturally supposed they belonged to the party that had fired the burning buildings. Whether they were members of Tall Bear's band or an independent body could not be told just then, and Melville had no time or inclination to puzzle himself over the question.

It was enough to know that he and his pony were in imminent danger, and that not a second was to be lost in leaving the spot.

He was in the saddle in a twinkling, and turned the head of Saladin to the north.

"A good deal depends on *you*," he said, patting the neck of the noble animal; "we have a rugged path to travel, and there isn't much chance to show them what you can do in the way of speed, but I know they can't beat you."

"To his dismay Melville observed that the bank was lined with mounted Indians."

I told you in the earlier part of this story that the upper trail, as it was called, was much more rugged and difficult to traverse than the lower one, which fact accounted for its general abandonment by those who had occasion to cross the stream. Had the ground for some distance been open prairie, Saladin would have shown a clean pair of heels to his enemies, and speedily borne his master beyond danger; but within a hundred yards of the bank of the stream the surface became so broken that it was difficult for a horse to travel faster than a walk.

But our young friend did not hesitate to assume the risk, and Saladin instantly broke into a canter, which, to say the least, was the equal in speed of any pace his pursuers dare attempt. The difficulty, however, was that the latter were already so close that a volley from them could not fail to do damage. The fact that they had some distance yet to travel through the water, where their ponies could not be forced off a walk, was a vast help to Melville, who improved the brief space to that extent that he was almost out of sight when the horsemen forced their animals up the bank and struck into a gallop.

Melville rode a reckless gait, which proved to be the wisest thing he could do; for, though Saladin came near stumbling more than once, he did not fall, and drew so far away from his pursuers that he soon left them out of sight. Satisfying himself of this, the youth abruptly drew him to one side, forced him among some rocks and bushes, faced about, and held him motionless.

"I don't know what has happened to Red Feather and Dot," he said, "and it may be they don't need my help; but I shan't do anything that looks like deserting them—*sh!*"

At that moment, the hoofs of the pursuing horses fell on his ear in his hiding-place, and he knew the three Sioux were at hand.

CHAPTER ELEVEN

AT THE LOWER CROSSING—TALL BEAR'S LAST FAILURE

NOTHING could have shown more strongly the confidence of Melville Clarendon in Saladin than the course he followed in trying to throw the pursuing Sioux off his track.

He had halted at a distance of less than fifty feet from the path, and, sitting erect on the back of the steed, he waited for the three Indians to ride past.

At such times a horse is quicker than its rider to discover the presence of other animals, and the temptation to make it known by a whinny or neigh has often upset all calculations and overthrown the plans of the fugitive or scout.

Melville knew the peril from this source, but he had little misgiving about Saladin. He softly patted his neck, and knew he understood the situation well enough to hold his peace; but how would it be with the other animals—would they betray their discovery of the motionless steed at the side of the trail? A faint neigh from them would be certain to give their cunning riders a clue to the truth; and, checking their own horses, they would leap to the ground, and be upon the youth before he could dash into cover.

You may understand, therefore, the anxiety of Melville when through the gloom he caught the dim outlines of the first horseman, as he came opposite, closely followed by the others.

The suspense was short. While the boy held his breath, the last of the three horsemen vanished in the gloom, and he was placed at the rear, with enemies on both sides of him.

The ruse of Melville had succeeded, and the question now to be answered was as to what use he should make of his opportunity, if such it should prove to be?

It would seem that nothing could be more reckless than for the youth, after eluding his three immediate pursuers, to return over the trail to the crossing, but only a moment's thought was necessary for him to decide to do that very thing.

"The last of the three horsemen vanished in the gloom."

From where he sat on his pony, screened by bushes and rocks, he observed that the light from the burning buildings to the south-east was fast diminishing. The fire had been rapid, and before long total darkness would rest on the stream and plain again. It would therefore be safe for him to approach the edge of the creek, provided none of the remaining Sioux had crossed over.

Waiting only long enough to make sure that the three Indians were beyond reach of the sound of Saladin's hoofs, he gently jerked the bit and spoke softly to him. The steed stepped forward with as much care as his rider could have shown, and soon stood in the path again.

Here Melville held him motionless a moment or two, while he peered around and listened. Nothing was seen or heard of the Indians, and, heading toward the stream, the horse advanced on a gentle walk.

Melville kept his pony at a walk for no other reason than to prevent any betrayal from the sound of his feet. The distance was slight, and soon he came to a halt on the very edge of the stream, while the rider, peering across, failed to catch the faintest outline of the horsemen that were in sight a short time before.

Nothing could have justified the risk of attempting to ride to the other bank; for if the Sioux were in the neighborhood they would not only discover the youth, but would have him at such disadvantage that escape would be out of the question.

The lad held no such purpose, but, turning his animal to the right, began making his way down stream, toward the Lower Crossing, near his own home. It was easy to do this by keeping close to the water, since the unevenness of the ground did not begin until a few yards or rods from the bank.

The darkness was such that Saladin was left to himself, Melville knowing he could give him no help by any attempt at guiding him. The sagacious beast thrust his nose forward, and, like an elephant, crossing the stream, seemed to feel every foot of the way.

Despite the extreme care, he had not taken a dozen steps when a rolling stone caused him to stumble, and the rider narrowly missed taking a header over his ears. Saladin quickly recovered himself, but at the moment of doing so the youth was startled by a whistle from the other shore, instantly answered by a similar call from the bank along which he was riding.

This proved that not only were the main party waiting, but the three Sioux that had started to pursue the young fugitive had returned.

But if the stumble of Saladin had revealed his whereabouts, Melville was still in great peril. Without waiting to assure himself on the point, he urged his pony to a brisk walk, never pausing until fully two hundred yards were placed behind him. Then, when he looked back and listened, he was convinced his fears were groundless, and it was a simple coincidence that the signals which startled him were emitted at the moment of the slight mishap to his horse.

So far as he could judge, he had a clear course now, and he allowed Saladin to advance as rapidly as he chose.

His chief distress was concerning Dot. The withdrawal of Red Feather was so sudden that some unusual cause must have been at the bottom. The lad could not help thinking the chieftain should have given him a hint of his course before the youth learned it at such a risk to himself.

He was not without fear that harm had befallen his beloved sister, but his confidence in Red Feather was perfect, and he knew that he would do his best to take care of her.

Convinced that the Sioux at the Upper Crossing were the ones that had fired the buildings to the south-east, and that they belonged to Tall Bear's band, it followed that something must have taken place to drive them from the siege of Melville's home.

It might be that, learning of the flight of the children, they had scattered to search for them. It would seem they were small game for such a big effort, but the ill success that had marked Tall Bear's brief career as a raider may have made him glad of even a small degree of success. Besides, it might be that only a portion of his party was on the hunt.

But to Melville the most likely belief was the one formed some time before, to the effect that company whose appearance had caused such excitement were white men numerous and strong enough to send the Sioux skurrying away to avoid a fight with them.

It was this belief which caused Melville to seek the Lower Crossing, when there was much risk involved in the attempt.

"If father and a lot of his friends have scared off Tall Bear and his Sioux, they can't be far off——"

"Climb down thar, pard, mighty quick!"

It was a startling summons that thus broke in upon the reverie of Melville, but he quickly recovered from the shock, knowing by the voice that it was that of a friend.

He had reached the Lower Crossing, when a horseman that was awaiting him suddenly loomed in sight through the gloom, and hailed him with the rough command to dismount.

"I don't see why I should get off my horse when he isn't stolen," replied the youth with a laugh.

"Wal, to be sure, if it isn't young Clarendon! Hello, Archie, here's your younker (boy), sure as you live."

It was the famous scout Nat Trumbull who spoke these cheery words, and, before the youth knew it, it looked as if a dozen horsemen had sprung from the ground and surrounded him.

"We're looking for Injins," added Nat; "thar was plenty of 'em a while ago, but they've become powerful scarce all of a sudden."

"I've seen more than I wished," replied Melville, "but I guess, you've frightened them off——"

At this juncture the boy's father rode hurriedly forward through the group, and, leaning from his saddle, gratefully pressed the hand of his son, and anxiously asked about Dot.

The youth, as briefly as he could, told the story which is familiar to you. The amazement of the listeners was great, and to more than one it seemed impossible that the detested Red Feather should have proved himself a friend instead of the most cruel enemy of the children.

"Why, it's him that we war after more than any one else," said Nat Trumbull; "but if he's made a change like that, why I'll shake hands with him and call the account squar."

Mr. Clarendon's distress over the uncertainty about Dot was so great that the thoughts of all were turned toward her; and when he asked that an effort should be made to trace her and Red Feather, Nat and the rest gave their eager consent, and the start was made without a minute's unnecessary delay.

Nat Trumbull was disappointed because of his failure to locate Tall Bear and his band. The outbreak of the Sioux was so sudden that even those who were best acquainted with their ways did not believe it was so near, but when the truth became known the authorities saw the only right course to take.

There were many hundred Sioux within the boundaries of Minnesota at that time, and unless the revolt was suppressed at once and with a strong hand it would rapidly spread, with the most lamentable consequences. There was a hasty organization and gathering of forces to start after the raiders and bring them to terms before they should gain courage by any important successes.

It was the ardent desire of the rangers under Trumbull to force Red Feather and his band into a fight where there would be no getting away on either side. The scout meant to hit hard when he did strike.

This statement will make clear the course of the irregular cavalry—as they may be called—when they became aware that the Indians whom they were after were gathered around the home of Archibald Clarendon. That gentleman was eager for himself and friends to dash forward, but Nat reminded him that the presence of the Sioux and the fact that, although the barn was a mass of ashes and smoking ruins, his house stood intact were proofs that the raiders had been unable to burn down the cabin or secure his children.

Such being the case, Trumbull began manœuvring with a view of getting matters in such a shape that a fight would be certain. There were several glasses among the rangers, and in the deepening darkness they gave important aid.

It was evident from the manner of the Sioux that they were not sure of the identity of the horsemen. Could they have used spy-glasses like the white men, they could not have failed to learn the truth.

Trumbull turned this uncertainty to his own advantage. He purposely held his men back to prevent the truth becoming known; but as the darkness increased he kept edging to the southward, spreading the horsemen out to an extent that would have proved costly had the Sioux been sagacious enough to take advantage of it.

Nat's force was too small to attempt to surround the Indians, and he was still hopeful of forcing them into a fight. He did not lose a minute, but worked farther and farther along, until all were far from that part of the horizon where first seen.

"Pressed the hand of his son, and anxiously asked about Dot."

But while Nat Trumbull was vigorously pushing things, it became known that two of the Sioux were hovering near and watching every movement. That these fellows were wonderfully cunning and quick was proved by their escape when both were charged by the horsemen. Despite everything that could be done, these scouts made off, and of course carried their important news to their chief.

The flight of the Sioux scouts caused a change in the plans of Nat Trumbull. Knowing it was useless to try to surprise the dusky rogues, he brought his men together and rode rapidly toward the Clarendon cabin. He hoped to arrive before the raiders could get away, and to administer sharp punishment to them.

Trumbull approached the house and smoking ruins with care, for there was abundant chance for their enemies to hide themselves and give the white men a rattling volley before they could escape the peril. It required considerable time for the rangers to learn that none of their enemies were there, and then Mr. Clarendon himself discovered the door of his house open. Still uncertain of the truth, he and his friends waited some time before daring to venture within.

The conclusion of this examination was the natural one, that the Sioux had fled, taking the children with them. But, as it was clear they could not have gone far, Trumbull galloped with most of his men to the crossing, in the hope of coming upon the marauders there.

He had no more than fairly convinced himself that he was in error again when Melville Clarendon rode up on Saladin, his father making his appearance shortly after.

The light in the south-east had attracted the notice of the scouts some time before, and the story told by the youth led Trumbull to believe the main body was near the Upper Crossing, where doubtless they had made Red Feather prisoner.

Accordingly, the dozen horsemen set their faces in that direction and struck into a rapid gallop. The leader was hopeful that, if the slippery scamps were located, he could reach them. He believed his men were as well mounted as they, and, if only a fair chance were given, they would compel the others to fight.

Nat rode at the head, with Mr. Clarendon and Melville just behind him. The keen eyes of the ranger peered through the darkness into which he was plunging so swiftly, on the alert for the first sign of an enemy. As he drew near the Upper Crossing he slackened his pace slightly, those behind doing the same, with the exception of the settler and his son, who found themselves at the side of the leader.

"Helloa! there's one of 'em!" exclaimed Nat.

The three saw the figure of an Indian running over the ground with great swiftness. Knowing his danger, he flung aside his blankets, so that his flight was unimpeded, and his exhibition of speed excited the admiration of his pursuers.

"Let him alone," added Trumbull; "I don't want any one else to interfere—he belongs to *me*."

And then, to the astonishment of every one, the scout made a flying leap from the saddle, and bounded after the fugitive on foot.

It was an odd chivalrous feeling which led him to do this. Inasmuch as the warrior had no pony, Trumbull meant that the contest between them should be without any unfair advantage to either party.

The Sioux was running like a deer, but the white man beat him. Nat Trumbull is to-day one of the fleetest runners in the north-west, and no doubt he felt a natural wish to show this Indian, as well as his own friends, what he could do in that line.

It may be said that from the first the fugitive was doomed; for if Trumbull should prove unequal to the task of running him down, the cavalry would do it, and if his strangely absent comrades should rally to his help, they would be fiercely attacked in turn. Since the white man quickly proved his superiority, it must be admitted that the outlook for the fleeing warrior was discouraging from the beginning.

Steadily and rapidly Nat gained on the desperate fugitive, until, in less time than would be supposed, he was almost at his elbow.

"Surrender, pard!" called out the scout; "for you don't know how to run, and I've got you, dead sure."

Realizing that there was no escape by flight, the Sioux dropped his rifle, and, whipping out his hunting-knife while still fleeing at the highest bent of his speed, he stopped short, wheeled about, and struck viciously at his pursuer with the weapon.

But the veteran scout was expecting that very thing, and parrying the blow with admirable skill, he sent the knife spinning a dozen feet to one side. Dropping his own gun, Trumbull then dashed in and seized the warrior around the waist.

"It's you, Tall Bear, is it?" said he, recognizing his old antagonist; "we'll settle this again by a wrestling-match. If you can throw me, we'll let you go without a scratch; but if I fling you, then you're mine. Keep back boys, and may the best man win!"

It was a curious scene, but the contest could not have been fairer. Trumbull waited till his opponent had secured his best hold, for Tall Bear was as quick to identify his rival as the latter was to recognize him.

The scout waited till the chief said he was ready. Then, like a flash, he dropped to a low stooping posture, seized each leg of the other below the knee in a grip of iron, and straightening up with marvelous quickness and power sent Tall Bear sprawling like a frog through the air, and over his head.

"Sent Tall Bear sprawling like a frog through the air."

Despite the remarkable agility of the Sioux, he could not save himself, but alighted on his crown with tremendous force.

Not the least amusing part of this contest was that, at the instant Tall Bear started on his ærial flight, he called out—

"Me surrender! Tall Bear good Injin—he lub white——"

The crash of his head against the solid ground checked his words, and left for ever uncertain what the chieftain meant to say. He quickly recovered from the shock, for possibly, it may be said, he was becoming accustomed to such rough treatment and could stand it better than at first.

In the course of a minute or two Tall Bear staggered uncertainly to his feet, and looking up in the faces of the horsemen who were on every side of him, was compelled to admit that he was their prisoner.

So it proved that the last essay of the chieftain who was on a little scout for himself was the greatest failure of them all, and in the end it was fortunate that such was the fact; for when the strong arm of the authorities was laid upon the raiders the chief had no trouble in proving that he had inflicted no serious harm to the settlers. True, he had destroyed some property, and tried hard to do greater damage; but, as I have said, he failed utterly.

CHAPTER TWELVE

CONCLUSION

BUT for his solicitude for Dot Clarendon, Red Feather never would have made the error he did, when waiting on the southern bank of the Upper Crossing for the return of the pony which was to carry them across to the waiting Melville on the other side.

The weather was still crisp and chilly, and, when he found himself alone, he began carefully gathering the blanket around the precious form, so, as to keep away all cold from her body. No mother could have handled her more gently. His left arm remained immovable, while his right fingered about her. He was quick to discover that she was in a sound slumber—a pleasant proof of the success of the grim warrior in the *role* of a soothing friend to the imperilled little one.

Softly raising a corner of the blanket, he looked down in the sweet face, which, though seen dimly, was as the face of an angel. Pure and holy emotions were stirred in that dark heart as never before that evening. He had parted his lips to utter something in his own language, when he was sharply reminded of his remissness by the clamp of horse's feet. Quickly replacing the blanket, he looked behind him, and saw outlined against the glare of the burning buildings the figures of six or eight horsemen, so close that it was useless for him to think of hiding or getting away.

Red Feather made no attempt to do either; for, like most of his people, he had a strong sense of dignity, which would have been disturbed by such action. His chief regret was that the horsemen had come upon him so suddenly that his action with the blanket must have betrayed, or at least raised a suspicion of, the truth. Had he but a minute's time, he would have gathered the covering about the form in such a way that in the darkness he might have kept secret the fact that he carried a small child in his arms.

His supposition was that these Indians were his own warriors; and a curious meeting must follow between them and the chief whom they thought dead, unless they had learned of his flight from the house, in which event a troublesome explanation must be made to them.

But the chief was pleased to observe that the men belonged to still another band, that had come from the south-east on their way to the Lower Crossing, in the hope of intercepting the settlers and their families fleeing in the direction of Barwell.

To use a common expression, Red Feather decided to "take the bull by the horns." He was well known and held in fear by all the warriors. He said he had captured a small child, stepping forward and parting the blanket enough for them to see her in his arms, and adding that he meant to take her home to his own wigwam as a present to his squaw. If the latter did not want her, he would put her out of the way, or hold her for ransom.

Had the new-comers possessed the courage, they might have asked Red Feather some troublesome questions, but they feared to rouse his anger.

He tried to keep their attention away from the other shore; but just then the glare from the burning buildings became so bright that he failed, and not only was Saladin observed making his way to that bank, but Melville was discovered as he rose to his feet.

Red Feather affected great surprise at the discovery, and offered no objection when the three Sioux set out to capture the lad and his valuable animal.

In the presence of these warriors Red Feather was his old, domineering, ugly self. He spoke sharply, and finally ordered one of the horsemen to dismount and give up his animal. He offered no theory to account for the appearance of the boy on the other shore, or for the singular fact that he was on foot himself.

The promptness with which his order was obeyed would have been amusing under other circumstances. Red Feather took possession of his property secured in this rather questionable manner, and then calmly awaited the return of the three who had set out to capture Melville and Saladin.

His fear was that the main party under Tall Bear might arrive and complicate matters; for the chief had formed the conclusion that the strange horsemen whose appearance allowed him to escape so easily from the cabin were white men, and that the main band of Sioux therefore had withdrawn.

By-and-by the warriors returned from the other side, with the announcement that the lad had escaped, and it was useless to follow him farther.

There was no chief with the smaller company, and Red Feather told them that, since there was no chance of finding any settlers in the neighborhood, they would ride back to their own villages, which lay to the south-east.

The start was made, and the horsemen passed fully a mile in grim silence. At the end of the mile he ordered them to keep the course they were following, while he alone turned to the right in quest of Tall Bear and his band of Muddy Creek Sioux.

Left to himself, Red Feather rode a short distance to the right, and then, changing his course due north, struck the pony into a gallop.

He was now heading toward the home of the Clarendons, where he had met so many singular experiences during the earlier part of the evening. He held Dot with such care that she continued sleeping as sweetly as if lying in her own bed at home.

Never was Red Feather more cautious and skilful. Thoroughly trained in woodcraft, and an adept in all the cunning of his people, he used those gifts with success, and, though he approached close to the party of Sioux which were hurrying away from the vengeance of the white men, they never suspected the fact, and the meeting was avoided.

Within the succeeding half-hour his listening ear caught the neigh of a horse which had detected his own while the two were invisible. Instantly the chieftain brought the pony to a standstill, and peered and listened with all the acuteness he possessed.

The horsemen were coming that way, and would soon be in sight. At the very moment their figures were beginning to outline themselves he emitted a whistle, precisely the same as that used by Melville Clarendon when he signaled to him from the Upper Crossing.

"The horseman were coming that way."

As he did so he held his pony ready to send him flying over the prairie at break-neck speed.

But his heart was thrilled almost in the same second by a reply, which he knew came from no lips except those of the boy himself.

Yes; Melville had recognized the call, and sending back the reply, he shouted—

"That's Red Feather! Come, father; I know he's got Dot!"

In a twinkling, as may be said, the chief found himself in the middle of the band of Nat Trumbull and his rangers, where he was overwhelmed with congratulations. Although Dot was asleep, her father could not be restrained, and caught her in his arms and pressed her to his heart with tears of joy and thanks to Heaven for its mercy in restoring her to him unharmed.

It must be said that Dot was disposed to be cross at being awakened in this summary fashion; but when her little brain came to understand all that had taken place, and she saw that it was her own father who was caressing her, she laughed and shouted, and wanted to kiss and embrace every one of the party, who were just as much pleased to fondle the child as though each had a proprietary interest in her.

Since it was evident the Sioux could not be brought to book, Nat Trumbull turned about and headed for Barwell, which the whole party reached before the morning sun appeared. Red Feather kept them company, and I must say that I doubt whether the President of the United States himself could have received a warmer welcome when the whole truth became known to the pioneers.

The outbreak of the Sioux was repressed before it had time to assume serious proportions, and, inasmuch as every one who had taken any part in it was anxious to clear himself, the leaders envied the position of Red Feather, who had faced about so early that no suspicion could attach to him. He was re-established in the good graces of his people, and since that time has acted in such a manner that no one will question his right to be considered a good Indian.

- 94 -

Milton Keynes UK
Ingram Content Group UK Ltd.
UKHW030911151124
451262UK00006B/832